STARLESS and Bible Black

by Gerard DiLeo

STARLESS and Bible Black
By Gerard DiLeo, © Gerard M. DiLeo, 2017…and *beyond*.

**To my nuclear and extended family
—the only stars I will ever need.**

Table of Contents

STARLESS and Bible Black

Prologue:
The Flicker—the Night the Stars Went Out

It was a beautiful, crisp, starry night blanketing the shadowed half of this predominantly religious world. The countless flickers, scintillating pinpoints of divine camaraderie, proclaimed our fellowship with the rest of creation. Too distant to render any heat, they bequeathed warmth in other ways.

They were our legacy, the stars. Our progenitors. We were in the continuum of stellar ontogeny, perhaps mere side effects; perhaps crowning achievements. Our dust was as germane to this continuum as the dust that made the stars that made us. We have lived as the progeny of fusion, depletion, collapse, and explosion, all forging elements heavy enough to become the sentient beings that wrote about them, first as myth, then romantically, and finally scientifically.

The twinkling night both chased behind and receded away from the day, the metronome by which all life on Earth bides time. For half of all of our heartbeats until the last, the gift of the night was ours to behold, allowing us to fall asleep in a comfort of constancy that our world would be there when we opened our eyes again. The repose that ended each day, when all brows unfurrowed and the beauty of infinite calm swept all faces, evidenced how we indeed were made in his image and likeness.

The sky dazzled those who looked up on this beautiful, crisp, starry night. It was cloudless, the curtains drawn away from center stage for the show that must go on. Night after night, since Man first looked up, this show was enjoying a good run. A million million points of light, often the metaphor for giving hope as it always had, promised an end—someday—to our loneliness: Were we first? Were we only? Were we left behind? The answers shined in staccato encryption on the dome of each night, awaiting meaningful dialogue.

Our large orbiting telescopes brought the beauty of the cosmos to the common man who financed it invisibly with withholdings from his earnings. There was a science called Astronomy, as richly explored as any other discipline. Cosmological certainties played the music of the spheres to those who danced with gravity and time and space, hoping to decrypt overtures from the aether. There was a pseudoscience called Astrology, as richly exploited as any other discipline. Cosmological alchemy played the music of the spheres to those who were tone deaf to the realities.

Astronomy looked outward, astrology inward. Outward, however, was where there were both hope and anticipation, beyond...perhaps, just perhaps...

The hope in the stars often slipped away, neglected and unappreciated, less and less on the minds of the distracted busy men and women otherwise going about their days that separated their nights; even children, who felt the hope more, only rarely fantasized the comic book possibilities of others elsewhere offering new ways that could change everything.

Mostly, life went on in our predominantly religious world, day after day, night after night, our stars unnoticed as much as the air around us; as much our companions as the love, hate, greed, benevolence, ruthlessness, and mercy that directed our motives and decisions. Always there for those ingrates who could simply look up, the stars faithfully held our hands in the universe whether we beheld them or not.

On a night we were to look up and see nothing, look up and see them no more, it would be a nightmare, just as intangible yet just as horrific.

We were not immune to nightmares, however. The astronomers at work at the eyepieces on our big telescopes financed by common men—on Mauna Kea, in the Canary Islands, and at Palomar—were having a bad night as their viewing opportunity drifted to them from the east at the speed of the world's rotation. On this one evening, for those astronomers who watched along serially darkening longitudes, the stars were gone. They had gone out. In a blink.

They simply were no longer.

No one guessed correctly the reason for their sudden disappearance, instead misdirecting blame on a suddenly overcast sky, on pollution, or even on washout by a greedy grandstander full moon which persevered as our only remaining friend in a universe previously filled with hope.

Motorized telescopes the world over moved more this night than in many years combined. But this—Shakespeare's *o'er-hanging firmament*—they discovered, was brave no more; this roof, they realized, was no longer *majestic* or *fretted with golden fire*.

The Saturn Encounter mission took the straight line into oblivion, no longer circling within the rings, because Saturn wasn't there. The New Horizons mission that had visited Pluto and now aimed for future Kuiper belt targets went astray into nothing. Martian rovers stopped sending data. The historic Voyagers I and II, now forever only moving away toward nothing, would never reach anywhere at any time, ever.

Astronomy ended that night. Astrology ended that night. Hope and anticipation ended that night. The Earth jutted out as a crag overhanging a sterile abyss. The sky was universally starless over cities like New York, Paris, Moscow, Beijing, and Llareggub. The sky was evenly Bible black over bucolic forests like Sherwood, the Sequoias, and Milk Wood.

Just as we outlast our nightmares, extinguished by each dawn, we all are only one sunset away from the nightmare's return.

The Journalist

The morning after the stars vanished, the daily goings-on went on more slowly for everyone. Anyone within sight or earshot of media soon learned of the mysterious and unsettling upheaval of the stars' disappearance.

Martin Bragg, the well-known journalist with two Pulitzers to his credit, abandoned his plans for his assignment that day. The whole world was dizzy because of the sudden absenteeism of things that didn't seem to affect them in any way whatsoever their entire lives; but taken away, there were fretting, confusion, hopelessness, and a great questioning of faith in this predominantly religious world. There was the sudden burden of sadness, also, which no one could put into words. And there was fear that we were next in line for erasure and it was probably coming soon.

"JPL," announced the Jet Propulsions Laboratory receptionist. Martin had called his friend's private mobile phone, but Dr. Lewis must have had it call-forwarded to his office line. The receptionist's voice was quite unreceptive, a monotone, disconnected and disinterested. Was it because of the stars, he wondered. Or was she always like this because she had never bothered to look up at the sky?

"Dr. Lewis, please," Martin Bragg asked politely. The receptionist didn't respond to him but delivered him sterile music originally controversial forty years earlier. Sex and drugs were Musak'd for his short wait for Dr. Michael Lewis, his old roommate from college. They had been buddies then and continued to be friends in the ensuing years. Their wives knew each other and their children knew each other. He remembered fondly their philosophical conversations back in the dorm room, each emblematic of their respective majors. Martin always cited from a literary or theological point of view and Michael from the scientific.

"Martin!" Dr. Lewis greeted him. "I think I might know why you're calling. Does it take the universe disappearing to get you to call?"

"Mike, what's happened?" Martin asked his friend. At first there was a silence, then Dr. Lewis stammered a bit.

"We, uh, don't know. We're stunned."

"Can I drive down to talk? Off the record if you'd like."

"It doesn't have to be off the record, Martin. There's nothing to say. We just don't know. And how are you going to make it to D.C. in time for the President's speech tonight if you're stuck on the I-5?"

"Don't worry about me. I'm coming down anyway. I'll be there in an hour."

"So soon?" Dr. Lewis asked.

"No one seems to be traveling right now. Everyone's freaking out. No one's going to work. The Freeway's empty. I won't be stuck on anything."

"Well, I'm at work, but maybe not for long if there's nothing out there to see anymore."

"Yea, I'm at work, too, which is why I'm coming. Bye."

"Bring a gun, Martin," Dr. Lewis said, and then replaced his telephone receiver in its cradle gently. He was much more than stunned by the empty sky, as his friend Martin Bragg would soon discover. The JPL engineer, also a theoretical cosmologist, felt an overwhelming sense of guilt and embarrassment over his inability to offer any type of explanation. And if he, one of the foremost stellar astronomers, was overwhelmed, he could only imagine what the uneducated—or even the educated laymen and laywomen—were feeling. Maybe a gun was an overreaction. Maybe it wasn't.

Martin Bragg, as promised, was there within an hour. The freeways were strangely idle, which made the pulled-over road rage duels more noticeable. He witnessed three shouting fights on the shoulder and two actual fistfights. It was funny how the mind worked, Martin thought. Why were those out more irritable? Or was it just that those who couldn't duck employment responsibility were just angrier than those who could afford to take the day off out of fear of an unknown universe? In any event, he drove very politely, unarmed, realizing the gun was not an overreaction.

Dr. Lewis was still in the same building and the same office. Martin saw the receptionist with whom he had spoken, who without eye contact or engagement waved him into Dr. Lewis' office with a lackluster movement of one hand. Martin entered and saw Dr. Lewis at his desk. His back was to a wall of journals, some shelves forgotten, others with dust-free piano-key drag marks where he had pulled out books recently. Martin sat down across from him at the front of his desk and held out his hands, opening both his palms to him, ready to receive anything Dr. Lewis had to offer.

"My best explanation?" Dr. Lewis said to Martin. "My best explanation is that a very large, dark molecular cloud is just passing through. There are large ones—light years big—that look like just empty space in the middle of galaxies."

"I see," said Martin, who was already formulating the headline for his article. He took out a small recorder and laid it on the desktop and pulled a small pad out of his pocket and began to write in it with a pencil.

"That was simple," Martin said. "What a relief. Pulitzer number three, here I come."

"I said my best explanation, not the right explanation."

"Well, shit. I guess that was too good to be true." Martin flipped his notebook closed and put it back into his pocket. He left the recorder where it was.

"The big problem with the cloud is that we should have seen it coming, a blind spot that could be seen approaching. I don't know any way we could have missed that."

"So your best explanation is a big lie?"

"Our best lie, Martin."

"What about some sort of polarizing filtering phenomenon?" Martin asked him.

"You mean, like from ozone or something like that?"

"Yes."

"Ozone," Dr. Lewis laughed. "Martin, leave the science to us, O.K.? Besides, the Moon would be funny-looking, but it isn't. Whatever has happened has done its trick well beyond the Moon."

"What about the planets? Saturn, Mars, the rest?"

"They're gone, too. Just gone. Like they never were. No asteroids, no comets, no nothin'."

"Wouldn't we feel that? I mean…all the planets must have some gravitational effect on the Earth…the tides…us?"

"Well, maybe if you're a Hollywood scholar of the Aztecs. And with all due respect to astrologers, no, Martin, not a thing. No effect on us, even if they were to all align, and that doesn't happen because they all tilt on their own ecliptics. But even if they did, the combined effect of all of them is over fifty times weaker than the Moon's effect. Now if the Moon took off, then you'd see some changes."

"They never align?"

"The odds are so low, it is much more likely the sun will die of old age before that happens—about five billion years from now. By that time, I really won't care." Dr. Lewis looked down. Martin studied his friend's face. He noted a collusion of forehead wrinkling, brow squinching, and grimaces that exposed a hint of panic.

"What about now, Mike? Do you care now? And I'm not talking about job security, either. I'm talking about the spookiness of it all."

"Spooky! Yes, that's the word. I was searching for how it makes me feel, and that's exactly how it does." He paused, and the conspiracy of facial movements further underscored his alarm. "So let's see…the Mars orbiter is flying crazy, because there's nothing to orbit. The rovers are MIA. Saturn Encounter kept sending us just a lot of black pictures until its broadcasts went spraying all over the place—no Saturn to go around. Even the asteroids being tracked for Near Earth Surveillance are gone. Martin, yes, I really do care. I'm spooked. And I care that I am very frightened, and now I suppose it's my job to come up with something so everyone else won't be frightened."

"What exactly are you frightened of? And why? And should I be, too."

"The molecular cloud," Martin told him.

"You're frightened of the molecular cloud? You said that was a lie."

"No, I mean, I like the molecular cloud as the explanation. It's wrong, but we've got to throw something out there. It looks like we're gonna go with that." He tested his liar's face. "It's a molecular cloud."

"And the truth?" Martin asked.

"The truth," Dr. Lewis answered, "is that they're really all gone. Not hiding, not misplaced, not masked in some way, but gone. Actually gone. All the stars. The planets. The works." He sunk back into his chair and shook his head. "Not the Moon. How come not the Moon?" he asked no one and everyone.

"How can you be sure they're really all gone?" Martin asked. "Maybe there's an explanation you haven't discovered yet. You don't even know what dark matter is. Maybe there's a bunch of dark matter around us."

"It's not dark matter, Martin. Put that in the same file as the ozone.

"Alright, Mike, just don't laugh at me again."

"Sorry. Look, there are new perturbations in the moon's wobble, the sun, and the Earth that indicate the rest is gone. The numbers are very small. Subtle. Like I just said, there's no significant gravity effect from the rest of the solar system, but there is enough to show that we're all alone now."

"The astrologers will all go crazy."

"Not just the astrologers, Martin."

"But if the sun is a star, why didn't it disappear."

"You might just as well ask why did Venus and Mercury disappear, too."

"I don't get you. Why shouldn't they? They're planets like the rest."

"Yes, but their orbits are between the Sun and the Earth. Even if there were some cataclysm that explains this that spares the Sun and the Earth, then everything in between should have been spared. They're all a package deal. But they weren't spared. Those two planets shouldn't be gone, too. But they are."

"And if they are, how come not the Sun with them?"

"Yes, and the Sun with them. Exactly."

"Let's revisit this alignment business again. Are — were — all the planets except the Earth on the same side of the Sun when this happened? That would explain how only the Earth got spared — the Sun, too — and how everything else was not spared."

"You're talking everything outside of the radius of one astronomical unit with all the other planets on the other side of the Sun? Yes, you're talking alignments again and, more specifically, complete or incomplete superior conjunctions."

"If you say so."

"Same problem with the odds. Besides, they weren't arranged that way. They were all over the place that night."

"Or day?"

"The folks on the other side of the world didn't see the stars' exit delayed by twelve hours. They disappeared on the day side, too, at the same time."

"They could see that?"

"Daylight makes it a lot harder, but with telescopes, yes. And there's Venus, the "morning star" on one side of the Earth and the "evening star" on the other side — it disappeared at the same time as both."

"Mike, we're governed by the laws of physics. I imagine a remote control would seem like magic to a caveman. We just haven't figured it out yet, that's all. Someone's going to have to figure it out, and it's not going to be me, obviously. I would say that your job security is very strong right now." Dr. Lewis began shaking his head in resignation.

"It's difficult," Martin, my friend, "to come to any other conclusions other than this was meant just for us."

"Meant just for us? By whom...or what?"

"Well, I don't think there could ever be any technology advanced enough to extinguish all of the universe except for us, our moon, and our star."

"You mean God, don't you? You're saying God did this?"

Dr. Lewis sighed. "Who knows? And I haven't even begun to talk about the problem of all of them disappearing at once. One has to consider the different distances all of the stars were from us."

"Go on."

"Well, for all of the stars to go out at once, they each would have had to do it at different times to coincide as the total blackout delivered to us, here on Earth, at the same time. A star a thousand light-years away would have had to burn out a thousand years ago, but one a million light years away would have had to burn out a 999,999 years before that. Now multiply that coincidence by the trillions and trillions of stars there are, well...I wasn't a religious man before last night, Martin, but I do believe that it's possible this comes only from God."

"Wow," Martin whispered to himself. "You're a scientist, though, Mike. You told me to leave the science to you, and here you go invoking God."

"I know," Dr. Lewis admitted, "so you would think I would have to do better than that. But I can't."

"But how could even God do this?" asked Martin, noting the irony that their original dorm room postures of long ago had reversed. "How could God do it without some magic?"

"God's God," answered Dr. Lewis.

"And that's your scientific explanation?"

"Well, I suppose the singularity could have been designed originally, fatefully, to bang, then inflate in such a way as to create all the stars with pre-designated life spans. Or maybe we've had it wrong all this time and the singularity wasn't the beginning, but the end, and outside of time they're the same." Martin gave Dr. Lewis a skeptical look.

"And you want me to put that in an article that everyone can understand? Look, Mike, what about the planets? They don't just burn out. What about the new stars? We ourselves come from new stars that have inherited the heavier elements, right?"

"They could have been...hmm...y'know, Martin, I don't know. But the only thing natural that could have presented like this is a large molecular cloud throwing a shroud in front of everything else beyond the moon. But then, why just surround us and the moon? And why do we still see the sun?"

"Still trying to sell the molecular cloud, I see. Well, maybe it could be surrounding us, the moon, and the sun."

"Now we're back to Venus and Mercury. Everyone will be screaming about them. They're the spoilers in that explanation. Real bugaboos. With gravitational indices indicating there is no Venus, no Mercury, everyone will jump on that pretty quick. Why can't our telescopes see them? Mathematically, you just can't reconcile that the Sun's there and Venus and Mercury ain't."

"*Ain't,*" Mike?

"I guess I don't care how I sound now. Listen to me...," he trailed off to himself, "*God.*"

"And *ain't.*"

"Yea, well, they used to be the same thing before last night."

"Could it be that the molecular cloud thickened up everywhere, even with us in it, and it's just that the Moon and the Sun are so bright that we can still see them through it?"

"I guess it could be that and all about their luminosities, but then the analyses on the light from the Moon and Sun would be different. You might as well bring up the ozone again. Their light would be polarized in a way that could be detected. We checked that already."

Martin paused his recorder. "I've been recording this. Hope you don't mind. I won't use any of the God stuff, but I want to get a statement now."

"God stuff," Dr. Lewis chuckled. "What I fear, Martin, is...what if this is God turning out the lights as he's leaving? That's the scary part."

"Is that your statement?" Martin asked.

"Oh, no. No, no. God, no. Certainly not. I'm still supposed to be a scientist, for God's sake."

"Damn," joked Martin, "imagine the headlines."

"Exactly," Dr. Lewis said back. "Good for you and bad for me." He defocused and mused out loud, "Molecular cloud, yes."

"How long will you be able to get away with that before the first indignant scientists blow the whistle?"

"Probably about a parsec."

"I thought that was a distance."

"Yea, it is. It's a Star Wars joke, Martin. Please excuse me, I'm going home. I know it's still there."

"Jokes, Mike? I want a statement I can use, not a joke."

"How 'bout both? Use this: the joke's on us."

The President of the United States

"Thank you, Father," President Edward Mason said. "Sorry I called you so late. And pray for me, even if I am a Mason." No one laughed on the other end of the line. The Vatican was a tough room.

He hung up the phone and sat quietly in the Oval Office, considering very carefully what the Director of the Vatican Observatory had to say. It had been an exhausting day, beginning with a rearrangement of his entire day to deal with the crisis the universe had handed him. The irony was that it was a most sensational crisis of no substance, a crisis of mist, a boogieman.

All we have to fear is fear itself. At no other time was this more applicable. How stupid he must have seemed to the Vatican scientist with his stupid Mason joke.

The day after the stars went out he had spent more time on the phone than not, speaking with Nobel Laureates, Pulitzer Prize recipients, NASA researchers, MIT professors, and even a JPL engineer one wall away from where Dr. Lewis and Martin Bragg were meeting. He had spoken with doctors from the CDC and the WHO and with the Surgeon General. He talked with his wife and children. He had called the men and women who were running Russia, Germany, Great Britain, France, China, Canada, Australia, and Brazil. And now he had capped off the discussions with the priest at the Vatican.

That evening he sat in his ready room adjacent to the Oval Office. He could hear the commotion of camera mounting, tripod adjustments, and audio checks through the door. He had with him his three advisors who continued to advise, but he was conflicted about the advice.

"I don't like it," he told them.

"It's the right speech, Mr. President," said a thin man without hair.

"I agree," agreed the man with hair.

"Me, as well," said the hard-faced woman.

At times insistent, at times obsequious, these three had been his voice of reason for Taiwan and a dozen other crises. His leadership, based on their advice, had saved the day each time and had paved the road to his re-election in November.

"It is not the right speech," he told them, but to the thin man without hair in particular.

"Well," the man responded, let's talk."

"Yes," said the hard-faced woman. "Let's go through it line by line. It's the only place you're ever going to get line-item veto."

"Very funny. Look, it's the entire theme. We're blowing this thing off. I agree that nothing has changed here, but we have to acknowledge the magnitude of it all. This speech says for everyone to just go about their business. Nothing happened. That's it?"

"Nothing has happened," said the woman.

"No, something very colossal has happened. Have you noticed? People have noticed, in case you weren't aware. They're freaking out. They want to know if the Earth is next. They want to know why. We've become so spoiled, I suppose. Breakthroughs buried on page twenty-three. The Higgs particle took two days to climb the charts before it was headlined on the front page. Discoveries mentioned in passing. This is a front-page story out of the gate, and you want it on page twenty-three under some celebrity bullshit."

"All we're saying," said the man without hair, "is that GNP must continue. You yourself had to close the stock exchange today. That was leadership."

"That wasn't leadership," the President corrected him. "That was common sense. I find imminent financial collapse pretty uncomfortable."

"You mustn't come off as freaking out, yourself, Mr. President. Leadership. Lead," answered the man without hair.

"Who do you think you're talking to?" he asked sternly with a leadership scowl.

"Sorry, Mr. President. Look, it's all on the teleprompter. You practiced it, right?"

"I looked it over, briefly. Don't like it."

"Well," said the woman, "too late to change it now."

There was a polite knock at the door, a knock as demure as the petite, young woman who did the knocking. She peaked in tenuously.

"Mr. President, it's time for your make-up. May I come in?" She was quiet as a mouse when she entered. Every movement was based on testing permission. Only her moving set her apart from the background. Her clothes hung on her, drab, uncolorful, and curve-defeating, her hairstyle brushed unimaginatively, her scent store-brand soapy just short of a sneeze, but her makeup was perfect: she was a specialist.

The three advisors stepped out of the room, satisfied that the speech was "in the can," as they liked to say. The cosmetologist set up next to the President's chair that sat behind his grand sweep of desk. He swiveled his chair to face her.

He was happy to see that it was the same young lady he had remembered from one of his campaign debates. He didn't always have the same makeup artist, but he remembered this one, because she had been the one who had given him the affable, honest face that very likely was responsible for an extra twenty-four electoral votes. That's what Vanity Fair had claimed, citing his stage presence as shrewd show business savvy while ignoring the cosmetician who was the real hero. They said it was his persona that night that put him over the top and made him President. He thought that maybe it was, thanks to her: she had subtly lined his jowls to create the solid square jaw of authority; her brushes and shades had given him the affable, sincere face of a father figure; his eyes had been opened with an enthusiasm for the world, thanks to just the right amount of liner, making them inviting windows for the voters. Yes, he thought, here, on his team, was a master artist.

Had her makeup really gotten him the Carolinas? Maybe so. Had a cosmetologist changed history? Maybe so. He thought of the global decisions he had made. The President had changed history and she had helped him into that position. He chuckled.

"What is your name again?" he asked her.

"Colleen, Mr. President," she answered.

"What do you think about all of this?"

"The stars, you mean?"

"Yes."

She dabbed here and there to reduce the albedo of his nose. Couldn't have a nose like that. The powdery fallout nearly made him cough. She paused for a moment after she was satisfied with his nose and looked down nervously when she spoke. "What do I think? Mr. President, what's a cosmetologist compared to the universe?" she asked tentatively.

"Or compared to the President?" he answered back. He let circulate for one pass in his brain the fact that there were only two letters difference between cosmetologist and cosmologist. The 1% difference in DNA between humans and chimps he let pass twice. The obvious perspective was laughable: the universe easily dwarfed the Presidents, CEOs, cosmetologists, lawyers, doctors, Ayatollahs, ditch-diggers, and all the other chimps who shared one very narrow band of self-importance in all of creation. On a truly objective scale, was there any difference between the leader of the free world and the makeup artist who made him that?

"Oh, no, sir, you're very important," she answered. "I mean, like, you're the President. I'm nothing, really. The world's not gonna change because of me. You, on the other hand…"

"In a way, I suppose I am very important…at a certain level." He picked up the telephone receiver and spoke in a whisper. "Everyone ready?" He looked back at Colleen. "We're finished here, right?"

"Yes, Mr. President. Break a leg." She suddenly realized what she had said and gasped.

"Don't worry," he told her, patting her on her hand. "I won't have the NSA after you for threatening the President," and he smiled at her. He prepared to speak into the phone again but he was in the next room, so he really didn't need to. "I'm ready!" he called out loudly from his Oval Office. From behind the doors came a collective sigh of relief.

"Two minutes, Mr. President," said his Press Secretary as he walked through the double doors alone into the flurry of lights and cameras that had staked claims throughout the room. One more afterthought dollop of makeup landed on the President's face within a moment, with Colleen dutifully blending it in. She gave his face a final appraisal and then backed away. The afterthought had paid off.

"Five, four, three..." said a young woman in heels, followed by the conclusion of her countdown, signed by hand. He looked around the room silently, and he might as well have been looking around the entire nation, who looked back at him. He saw his wife holding their infant daughter and wondered how she would come of age and where she might end up in a starless world.

"Turn off the teleprompter," the President ordered just before the countdown ended.

"Oh, no," said the countdown woman under her breath. Reluctantly, the false ink of the teleprompter faded from the screen. He had done this before. Twice. The first time was during the Taiwan crisis, also called the Final Taiwan Straights Crisis, even though everyone knew there would be another. The second time was during the hostage crisis during the San Diego Special Olympics. Each of those times the polls said he did better without his teleprompter, personifying sincerely the actual leadership that otherwise lurked quietly under the budget concerns, partisan background noise, and jockeying for polling results. He did a silent count to three himself and then spoke. He appeared expressionless, unless one were to look at only his eyes as he spoke.

"Mr. Vice President, all Americans, all the world, I greet you not as a world leader or a politician, but as a citizen of Earth and a concerned member of the human race. The startling inability to see anything beyond our Moon except our own star has stirred strong opinions and emotions from astronomers, theologians, and even psychiatrists. Our star appears to be alone for as far as we can determine, out through the vastness of space. Unfortunately, jeopardizing our peace of mind is that none of these experts, scientists, or philosophers can personally offer a reasonable explanation, let alone a guarantee of a correct one.

"As a nation, we Americans have been tested many times. Two world wars, many regional wars, a depression and several recessions, struggle and victory over segregation, and painfully learning from mistakes made—on land, in the air, in space and in our attempts to get there—we have always been at our best when things were worst. That reference, deliberately, is from a movie—a story about a man from the stars."

He paused for effect, but it was for him, not his audience. Post-production archivists scrambled to text their assistants to identify that particular movie for insertion into the polished report that would be forthcoming.

"I have conferred with many learned men. As a religious man, I admit that all of this has the same faith-challenging results in me as it may have caused in you. I have just ended a phone conversation with a Jesuit priest, Father Racivitch, the current Director of the Vatican Observatory. Since it was hard to separate all of the mixed religious, astronomical, and fatalistic feelings, I called him as your President, because I can; and I called him as a man, because I had to. Earlier this afternoon I spoke with astronomers at the Jet Propulsion Laboratory and NASA. I have spoken to a great many people since last night. I have also noted well every conversation I had in between my calls with people from all walks of life I had encountered. Chefs, drivers, my personal physician, and many others. The thing that has struck me is that they don't expect an explanation from the learned men and women I consulted. The sense I get from them is that what has happened is bigger than even experts.

"Father Racivitch assured me, as did other religious leaders, that this is no act of retribution or omen that retribution is imminent. But the Vatican goes beyond relying on a loving God, scientifically assuring me that this is a phenomenon that can be explained. There is no such thing as magic, I was told, and it would have to be magic for something like this to actually be what it appears to be. Many are hard at work to discover what has happened. And we will find the answer. I have no doubt that a Nobel Prize awaits the one who makes this discovery.

"I look up and see nothing except our last remaining companions, the Moon and the Sun, just like you. I wonder what has changed, as do you. And like you, I cannot explain the unsettled feeling I get, even though I know the stars have never directly affected me before, nor can their sudden absence directly affect me now. But unsettling it is. If the Mona Lisa, The Pietà, the Taj Mahal, or the Grand Canyon were to suddenly disappear, it would be unsettling as well, but something tells me that I would get over it. Eventually." He smiled at the political downside of losing his support in Arizona, as if that mattered now.

"But I know that anyone who has grown up with stars overhead may find it difficult to get over this. Perhaps the generation born, beginning today, may be free of the unanswered anticipation we, all born before their disappearance, feel when we do not see what we have been nurtured to see when we look up, as much a part of us as up is up and down is down. As imprinting on us as the faces of our mothers when we nursed as infants." He pulled a scrap of paper, unfolded it, and read.

"An American artist, Laurie Anderson, spoke these words:

'... the reason I really love the stars is that we cannot hunt them.
We can't burn them or melt them or make them overflow. We can't flood them or blow them up or turn them out.
But we are reaching for them...'

"And this is what is unsettling. We seem to have nothing to reach for, and that is vexing. Nothing to strive for. Answers, sought out with such curiosity and intensity, now have no questions. It is tempting to think we are on our own, and this will be our greatest test—the test within ourselves. As a man, I share this discomfort with you. As your President, I implore all to look around at your loved ones, your worldly ambitions, and your own sense of inherent self-worth, and know that what you see and live *is* the meaning of life… not the stars, wherever they are. I implore you to wake up at the usual time and go to work, be it homemaking, agriculture, science, or any of thousands of vocations and callings. The worst thing we can allow is a malaise that this means something to us as human beings. We are not alone. Look around. Life is a great gift, and we know it exists here, and we have never been able to prove it exists anywhere else, anyway. So I ask you to get on with life as we know it. Even if we see it a bit differently at night. Raise your new starless children like you raised your starry-eyed children. Raise them right. While we exhaustingly seek the reason for this phenomenon, life should go on. While we launch the great effort to rescue our stars from obscurity, living should continue." He paused, and sweeping his gaze at all in the room, he stopped at his daughter and smiled. He raised his head again to eye the journalists in the back of the room.

"In apology to the press corps, there will be no questions now, because to emphasize my very point, I have to get back to being the President. I'm busy, and so should all of you. I know all of you had plans. Follow them. God bless America…and all. Thank you and good night."

The high-heeled young lady who had initiated the telecast with her countdown now dragged her finger across her neck. The bright lights went out. The makeup that had been so emergently applied was now gently blotted off of the President's face.

"Plans, yes, plans, Mr. President. That was very inspiring," the makeup girl said as she worked to free his face of his maquillage. He thought of Eleanor Rygby, wearing the face that she keeps in a jar by the door. Who was it for?

"Thank you," he replied.

"Mr. President, if I may —"

"Sure."

"Thank you for that bill that offered homeowners that tax credit. That'll really help me on next month's mortgage bill."

"Well, it's not really a straight trade of—Eileen, right?" he asked her.

"Colleen, Mr. President."

"Oh, yes, Colleen. Sorry. You know, Colleen..." the President trailed off.

"Yes, Mr. President?" She was dizzy inside with the very idea that she was actually having a conversation with the President of the United States. This was a moment she could brag about to her children and grandchildren. Not the day after the stars went out, but the day she talked with the President.

"You know, Colleen..." he trailed off again.

"Yes, Mr. President?" she repeated.

"Colleen, if it's alright with you, I don't think I want to be President anymore."

The Evangelist

He was the last great Evangelist standing, the only one who hadn't yet been discharged from his duties via an adulterous tryst, an errant child out of wedlock, a financial malfeasance or discrepancy, or an underage or Biblically prohibited same-sex indiscretion. Yet, he was all these, and more. He had not been caught yet by anyone else but God; not even by himself.

He wrote his sermon as an answer to the President's message the evening before. This was the President who, after all, championed taking the word God out of his Pledge of Allegiance (previously under which our nation stood) and the word God out of his money (previously in whom we trusted). This is the President who finally completed the separation of Church and State by rescinding his tax shelter. This was the President who promoted the notion of same-sex marriage, third-trimester abortions, and drone attacks on U.S. citizens abroad if someone, so duly authorized, deemed them a threat to national security. This was the President who was anti-gun, although he claimed he was pro-Second Amendment. This was the President who had been divorced and remarried, and who had had affairs in both marriages.

This is the President who said just last night we have plans and we should follow our plans.

"Yes, we have plans," shouted the evangelist, referencing the President's inspiring speech. "Our plans, Mr. President, are to follow God right out the door."

He knew this might very well be his last sermon. Maybe he could last another month. Maybe not. He assessed his audience. There couldn't have been more than a hundred and fifty faithful there—his loudest champions, his poorest champions. But what crowd there was in the mostly empty auditorium erupted at his words and his commandeering voice.

"And just like God did, we're gonna turn out the lights on the way out." The small crowd, so small through attrition that they hardly covered cost for each service, erupted again. "And we're gonna lock the door on the way out, too, shutting in this wicked world."

"Lock 'em in! Lock 'em up!" a cry went out.

"This country—which used to be *our* country—took away our God, took away our prayer, took away our God-fearin' values and morality." Amens were shouted. "This country has allowed homosexuality, bestiality, incest, pedophilia, sodomy, and it has called it all alternative. Called it a normal variation." He paused a beat.

"A *variation? Normal?*" he asked his audience.

"No!" from the congregation.

"Imagine that! It has called those of us—who believe—names, called us stupid and asinine. Hollywood agrees. Rolling Stone magazine agrees. The New York Times agrees. And now the lights have gone out. Do you think the Lord is trying to tell us something?" He repeated it again, this time shouting.

"Do you — I ask — think he is trying to tell us something? I kinda think he is! I kinda think the Lord totally...completely...without doubt...disagrees with Hollywood and the New York Times!" Each time he said "he," he raised both arms in the air, making a capital "H."

The affirmations affirmed and the adorers adored. Halleluiahs resounded.

"Night before last I was not watchin' the stars go out. You wanna know where I was?"

"Tell us!"

"I was on my knees at my bedside, praying for this great country and all of you."

"Halleluiah!" they cried, followed by more affirmations, some of them spoken in tongues.

"And I thought I felt a presence." Now he whispered, "An evil presence." He spoke normally again. "So I prayed harder. For this great country and all of you. I looked up and saw him. I saw the devil."

"Fuck the devil!" a teenage girl shouted, who otherwise wore a Sunday-best demeanor of innocence. Audible gasps from the congregation for either the devil or the expletive.

The Evangelist stopped and looked in her direction. "Who said that?" he asked. Slowly, tentatively, the precocious girl raised a hand.

"I'm sorry," she said nervously. "But is it alright to use swear words if you're using them at the devil?"

He looked at her low cut dress. She was standing now, so he looked at her pretty legs. *Man, I'd like to —* he thought to himself lasciviously, then suppressed it. *Eighteen*, he pledged. *Must be eighteen.* Then he looked more closely at her. *Oh, I already have. Ha!*

"Yes, my lamb," he said to her and winked. She blushed. "Cursing the devil can never be wrong." She had been tense, but exonerating her allowed her to loosen up. She looked around and smiled at the tenuous looks of approval, and then she retook her seat in the pew. He looked up to Heaven when he continued.

"And I said, 'Be gone, devil, I pray you away!'"

"Amen!"

"But he didn't leave me. And I knew that God wanted me to represent, so I challenged the devil. And the devil said, 'What's the wager, Reverend?' And I said, 'my soul.' And then I said, 'What do you wager, devil?' and he said, 'All the stars in Heaven.'" More affirmations echoed.

"And we fought all night. Just like living the righteous life is a struggle with the Devil. And there were times when I thought I might falter. Like our great country has."

"No!"

"Yay-a, there were times last night where I thought I might lose my wager, like this great country did."

"You're better!" someone shouted, followed by several amens.

"So it only inspired me to fight harder. And harder. And harder!"

"As hard as it took!" someone goaded him, and there were affirmations upon halleluiahs.

"But I couldn't beat him."

"That can't be!" decried someone.

"I say unto you that as hard as I tried I couldn't beat that ol' devil. And I said, 'Be gone, devil. You can't beat me. I have the Lord on my side.'"

"Amen!"

"And Jesus. And the Archangel. And you, my followers."

"We're here! Be gone, devil!" Amens upon affirmations.

"But…I am sorry to say…that I'm a sinner. I didn't beat him."

"No. You're wrong!"

"Just like our great country didn't beat him." Gasps and denials. "But he just looked at me and laughed. ' I'm not the Devil, sinner,' he said."

"He was!" shouted a man.

"Who else?" shouted his wife.

"And that's when I realized he was right. It wasn't the Devil I was wrastlin', but the Lord Himself!" Gasps from below the pulpit.

"How could this be?" shouted another woman.

"And it wasn't me fightin', but our great country. You see, this great country has lost its soul. To the queers and the drug users, the gamblers and the drinkers, the profiteers and the superrich, the rapists and the illegals and the Hollywood stars."

"Fuck the Hollywood stars!" the teenaged boy shouted. A hush came over everyone. Cursing the Devil was one thing, but… And then the teenager was rescued by amens upon amens.

"And I'll tell you what the Lord told me."

"Tell us!" they shouted.

"He looked me right in the eye and said, 'I'm leaving.'"

"No! Please, no!" shouted his followers.

"Yay-a! He said, 'I'm leavin' an' I'm taking the stars with me.' And he did. He left! And he did take the stars with him. That's what he did, arright!" Then a silence fell upon the crowd, as if they knew they were busted, caught, found out — guilty.

"So look up. The Lord is trying to tell us somethin' and the Lord has spoken! And he's waiting for our answer. It's an emergency, I tell you."

"Tell us what to do!" an elderly woman spoke as loudly as she could, then broke into a hacking cough.

"Tell us how to answer him!" a young mother shouted past her baby at her breast.

"Money talks, my brethren. Be generous tonight. It's gonna take a lot of money to fight the whores, sinners, and Hollywood stars. Fightin' the Devil is expensive. I can't do it alone. Help me help you!"

The noise from the crowd went down an octave. He heard the murmurs and mistook it as a good sign.

Backstage he inspected the collection basket. Thirty-four dollars and twenty-two cents and a Canadian penny were not going to be enough to fight the whores, sinners, and Hollywood stars, much less the devil himself. It would hardly cover his next carton of Marlboros. He knew he had given his last sermon. He flipped the Canadian coin deftly into the trashcan in the corner of the room. He knew that God was indeed trying to say something, but it was to him.

Working in mysterious ways, however, God relegated the message to his prophets—Ernst and Young—for special delivery, because it wasn't just God trying to communicate with him, but the Justice Department, too.

As the crowds had dwindled each week, the ones who remained were the least capable of supporting their religious champion. That was only part of the message, however. Ernst and Young also sent him a check for $102,000, all he had left, their way of notifying him that they had closed his account.

But this was Department of Justice code: you're under investigation and indictments are soon to follow.

It was as clear to him as the stars departing had sent a message to a heathen nation. For as the last great televangelist standing, he had fallen down as fast as any falling star and would never rise again.

This evangelist had been discharged from his corporate duties, as he saw it, by God. And his retirement golden parachute was to be an express ticket to Heaven, contractually obligated to him by God, again, as he saw it. That it was a third-class ticket for a train that would take him anywhere but there, collected whilst on board by the bullet through his head, would come as the dirty trick he would never forgive.

For eternity.

The Philosopher

His wife finally moved out. She had always accused him of neglecting her, whether by having a book in his hand, a podcast through his ear buds, a journal on his tablet, or by sitting in front of his computer emailing irrelevant insights to colleagues. But in this new world, the one with no stars in the sky, she felt he had reached a new level of failing her. The change in the skies had provided fertile ground for him for new ruminations, and he could not waste any time on romance, love, or even meaningful communication at the supper table. He never left his laptop and his laptop never left him. He was smug about it being a Mac.

He wrote:

Now that the stars are gone, I worry about God. Not about God, actually, but about the concept of God. I feel the caveman looked up one night long ago and saw all of the starry sky, and then he created God. It was a natural connection. And maybe it was the other way around. Does it matter whether God created the stars or that the stars created God? I feel both are gone.

He had stopped eating with his wife long before the stars went out, but afterwards she had convinced herself that setting a place for just one was less wasteful and humiliating. When she finally left him, there was a place set for no one each evening. He didn't notice.

They hadn't owned a TV for years, since the onset of reality shows — the last straw. He was smug about that, too. His wife was a media widow nonetheless, as his other avenues toward philosophic enlightenment were competitive enough to make her want a real husband — one with a need for her, one who cared for her, one who cared for anyone or anything tangible. He who traded away existing for existentialism now neglected her even more loudly with his silent contemplation on the worn leather sofa-sleeper, often not leaving it for days except for bodily functions or a bite to eat. He sat on it and just philosophized, as if all of his experience, education, and training had been in preparation for the day the stars went away. He shared his epiphanies with his former university colleagues, who at one time had sucked up to him when he had been their Chairman. Now he was retired but was just as passionate, and he couldn't understand why many of his missives went unanswered. Was he no longer a player? He was insulted and hurt his colleagues did not respond to the pearls he offered them. He became bitter.

He wrote:

The stars have taken all propriety and dignity with them. We are no longer Venn diagrams, intersecting interestingly along these webs we weave. We have no circumferential border, all isolated sets oblivious to all of the other isolated sets. And it will only get worse, because that's what happens when entropy starts spreading all of the isolated sets even farther apart.

At night he slept on his worn sofa-sleeper, but only as a sofa, defying its definition by not even pulling it out into the bed that lay waiting for fulfillment. It was just as well, he mused only once, sealing its obsolescence: he feared what might be under the cushions.

He was therefore alone, mateless, academically ignored, and spurning functional furniture. He became divorced, although he had never bothered to go to the post office to sign for the registered mail that made it official. Once a week he walked out of his door and returned through it an hour later with a gallon of milk, two loaves of bread, and new pack of Oscar Mayer bologna. Once a month, he returned with replacement plastic bottles of mustard and mayonnaise and a new tiered pack of meat. Once a day, around 3 P.M., he left his sofa and made the bologna sandwich with mustard and mayonnaise on toasted bread, chased with a cup of cold milk. He was losing about a third of a pound a day. He perfectly expected to do this until his weight could no longer sustain him and he would die, joining the stars wherever they were.

The philosopher philosophized, writing:

The stars were our invitation to the universe. Even though we could not reach them, we did RSVP the invitation. We were planning to go. We penciled it into on our calendars, somewhere. But now we were no longer invited. The invitation has been withdrawn, revoked. We had ignored some RSVP deadline. We were no longer welcome in the universe.

What had we done to offend? What was it about us that made us so unlikable? Why were we so unwanted? How does one make amends to the infinite?

What we did to offend whomever, he philosophized, is that we probably committed hubris. He wrote:

It was more important that we go to the stars than it was that the stars receive us. Every true meeting is a mutual confluence of presence from approaching travelers, but we fancied ourselves to be the very meaning of that meeting. Our handshake would have the firmer grasp and it was lucky, for whomever, that we would finally be there.

What made us so unlikable was that we couldn't be our best until we had to. We never accomplished anything until we had to. That is what the President and that movie had said. And all of our noble accomplishments were tainted, as most of them came about because of wars, plagues, famines, or natural disasters. Or profit.

Our progress was dirty.

It kept a respectful distance from God. And the invention we wrenched from the evil stepmother of necessity maintained our resentment toward him.

We were so unwanted because first and foremost we want to get what we ourselves want, and then when there's an overabundance and the time, at our leisure others can get what they need if there is anything left.

The philosopher, between cups of milk and his bologna, became ashamed for humanity. He knew one could not make amends to infinity. He was a part of it, he realized, and all he had to show for it was some bologna.

He prayed.

He philosophized that his prayers went nowhere, like they all had probably gone in the past. They were just as open-ended on their journey into the aether as the TV signals that broadcast the affairs of today's celebrities, real housewives, scandal participants, and the publicist-sponsored superwealthy; behind the same waves that sent off the Zsa Zsas, Elizabeth Taylors, and Sinatras years earlier; the electromagnetic data that would enjoy no reception anywhere now.

At one point he fell asleep and didn't awake for three days. He found it amusing that after that, he still felt very tired. And then after that, he still felt very alone. He closed his Mac laptop, which had long since gone into sleep mode itself and its battery long dead. He was no longer e-communicado with the world. His mind began to drift.

To simple things.

He remembered long ago seeing a comedy about beer. He chuckled to himself over it. At one point in the movie, the two main characters had been driving down a winding hill and realized that someone had disconnected the brakes. The driver had let go of the steering wheel once he realized his brakes were out.

"No point in steering now," the feckless driver had said, which incited the passenger's desperate frenzy of leaping for control of the wheel.

He wrote:

No use even steering.

No one seemed to him qualified to take control of the wheel. Not Presidents, evangelists, media moguls, artists, astronomers, or even lovers who had not given up. Then he fell asleep again, because he was still very tired.

Tired of everything.

Sleep was his final desertion of the life outside his house that he despised. He wanted no part of the vanity that begged adoration of *cool*. He wanted no part of the new currency that was how many *likes* one received online. He couldn't abide the pop chart that defined culture, the put-downs that were the new wit, or the double-crossing one-upsmanship that was the new ingenuity.

Like a bear time-shifting away from winter via hibernation, he took the divorce from his wife a step further and called it quits with the rest of the world by sleeping. Lying in state, his brow unfurrowed and the beauty of infinite calm swept his face. He was no longer steering.

His chest rose and fell rhythmically. He was still alive. He just didn't know if he would ever wake up. But when he did, he would still be just as dead.

He wrote no more.

The Malaise

Humanity felt itself flexible enough to deal with such a surprise, boasting, *We are used to surprises. Earthquakes, tornadoes, hurricanes, global wars, pandemics — we dealt with those and we would deal with this. After all, the empty sky would not shake any buildings onto anyone or flood any cities; nor would it commit genocide, blow our houses apart, or be a vector for pestilence.*

The wave of discontent said otherwise.

The interchange between the sky and the soul, now severed, created a malady that was unmeasurable, then immeasurable. It did not pass from person to person or demographic to demographic, but from the empty sky to the soul, an emptiness that continued to empty all that it invaded.

There was still beauty in the world, because it remained as the standard against which all ugliness was judged. Pretty girls and handsome boys resisted unsuccessfully being hailed the beautiful people. Charity was alive and well, but only when tax-deductible. Music evolved and it still moved people, but atonality and backbeat pollution segregated those who listened from those who simply heard.

The pure of heart who steadfastly stood against the wave were called uncool, retards, and neo-Luddites. They were also called non-secular, the most vicious invective — fighting words everywhere.

Untethered to Creation, the devout of organized religions began to experience, for lack of a better term, a time-out as they re-evaluated the meaning and sacrifice of their devotion. This mutated into a defiant apostasy, although most said, instead, that it only had *matured* into an agnostic respite. The projections and extrapolations were constructed and they reported that within a decade there would be only 150,000 Catholics left, mainly the clergy who would persevere stubbornly for the sake of their sacred rituals, rites, and sacraments. There would remain only 220,000 Muslims, and even that estimate had been adjusted upward, since it was assumed that the great purge of apostates by Sharia Law execution would never occur. Except for Israel, there would be left only 8,000 practicing Jews elsewhere. There would remain no Protestants whatsoever. Non-denominational Christian projection was impossible to count, but would probably fall significantly from the pre-starless count, which was also impossible to count. The Mormon count that was projected would be only 150 — hardly enough to proselytize adequately in even one city — so wouldn't count at all. Scientology and Dianetics would be completely forgotten, but other cults would stand ready to step in. The Amish numbers wouldn't change, but the Amish never changed anyway. The Jehovah's Witnesses, it was predicted, would fall from eight million to only 144,000, which they claimed was just perfect.

Financial markets crashed the day after the stars went out. They recovered and then crashed again. They recovered yet again, but with a market correction that reset the averages and made billionaires millionaires and made millionaires start over.

Doomsday apologists, the only religious zealots who would persevere, began announcing Judgment Day on Bourbon St., in the Latin Quarter, in Rembrandtplein, on Kuta Beach, and in the Skadarlija district, Taksim Square, and Puerto Banus. Still no one took them seriously, but now no one laughed at them.

Mental quirks increased. Scientific journals debated whether there was an increase in the incidence of autism or whether there were just new subcategories, previously unrecognized, applicable to the spectrum. People began claiming they were seeing more ghosts than usual, attributed to a new anxiety state that had its own ICD code. Self-appointed Wise Men claimed to follow solitary stars no one else could see, again prompting another new ICD code. Suicides spiked, commonly from those becoming unemployed—NASA astronomers, for example, whose idleness trickled down the economy to lay off rocket scientists, aerospace engineers, aerospace construction workers, and the makers of parts the construction workers used, to wholesalers, retailers, and mail order venues for the durable goods needed for the laid off workers; from there to machinery manufacturers, farmers, maritime workers, laborers, and entitlement beneficiaries. Enmeshed in this tangled web of economic decline were the influences from the pessimism of all other walks of life, fueling the entire debacle as a breeder reactor.

Children were tested and demonstrated an underlying sadness. Cancer patients became more likely to give up their brave fights. And everywhere, with no clear explanation for what happened to the stars everyone came to realize they loved, there was an insidious fear building that nothing mattered. Crime increased.

Ecosystems faltered, effect begetting cause begetting effect on the life cycles of nocturnal species, in turn influencing all circadian life. The 17-year locusts would never re-emerge. Migratory birds would stake out permanent residences, giving up their nomadic lifecycle. The fishing industry was decimated in a complex, undecipherable interaction among dozens of species. Zoos became much too noisy and languished financially. Dogs didn't know what had happened, but they didn't care; cats did, but they also didn't care.

A novelty item, the household private planetarium projector, made a fortune for some, but the folks who used them all night were suspected of being conflicted in some way and were generally unpleasant to be around.

People became different, the change in the heavens responsible in some way. People quarreled more often and more viciously. Divorce became the expected, natural consequence of marriage; parenting suffered and delinquency increased. Psychiatrists and psychologists published erudite studies about all the changes in learned journals, but like most of psychiatry, it was speculation.

The next generation, the starless children, were expected to determine their own spirituality, hollow and portending poorly for the last churches, which would remain empty. Next, even the hollow personal spirituality would erode away, not even a shell remaining.

There was a lifespan, a life during it, and nothing after it. Self-indulgence became the authenticity of existentialism. It became wrong only to get caught doing wrong. Countless generations had evolved convolutions around the brain to suppress the amygdaloidal thinking of everyone's private reptile, but a life never having known stars engendered devolution. A new paradigm defined success, ambition, celebrity, and worth, inscribed on the caveman's walls and re-emerging in modernity as the One Commandment:

If you want it, you take it.

It easily replaced ten previously handed down from Mt. Sinai.

The Astronomer and the Astrologer

An astronomer and an astrologer walk into a bar…

The bars began having a good year the night the stars went out, filling with those who had previously filled the churches.

This particular bar, previously struggling, now made its owner a good living. It reached a point where he had to hire three more bartenders. *Who woulda thought?* he asked himself. *Lucky for me. She probably would have stayed if she'd known how rich I'd get.* He would look to the sky and say, "Thanks, fellas, for waiting till she left. Just gimme a heads up if you decide to come back. And if you do, don't bring her back with ya."

Bars that normally closed at two, or at midnight, or at some other last call countdown decreed by state law, were now allowed to stay open all night. Just because. No one had opposed the change. State by state opened the floodgates of alcohol to all that sought refuge from the gloomy, jet-black sky.

"But yours is junk science," the astronomer told the astrologer, lifting his glass and taking a sizeable swig of his beer. "Not real science. Not any science at all. Am I right?" He said it loud enough so that everyone was invited to answer.

"Absolutely not," the astrologer argued back. He took his own drink now and matched the astronomer's gulp, both mugs, again, with the same amount of remaining beer. "We're that and more. We are mysticism, with ties back to Christ and Josephus. We are Balthasar and the other astrologers from the East who followed a star." Now he led with a drinking challenge of his own, but the astronomer matched him right back with a gulp.

"Hmm...religion? You're using religion. Why do I feel you're not challenging my position very well?" The astronomer smiled smugly.

"At one time religion and science were the same," the astrologer pointed out.

"Yes," agreed the astronomer. They cleaved during the Renaissance, my friend, in what was also called the Age of Enlightenment."

"Actually, you stand corrected. It preceded the Enlightenment. It was the time DaVinci was imprisoned for his heliocentric position on the solar system. I wouldn't go bragging about the Renaissance."

"What about Copernicus?" the astronomer asked.

"Who's Copernicus?" asked the bartender. "Another round?"

"Yes," the astronomer and the astrologer said together.

"To heliocentrism," the astronomer said and clinked his glass with that of the astrologer.

"To the Music of the Spheres," the astrologer answered. Another clink.

"To Pythagoras," they both said together.

"Who's Pythagoras?" the bartender asked.

The conversation followed the pace of the drinking. Each point was made, followed by a counterpoint, and each set of gainsaying was punctuated by a lift of the glass and one mug catching up with the other. And each toast was followed by the bartender's ignorance and another offer for a refill.

"Another round?" the bartender asked again. And so it went, over and over. The man of science began slurring his expositions, and the man of mysticism began making more sense to him; the man of mysticism began using foul language, and the man of science began to listen more closely.

"I mean," said the astrologer, "you fucking scientists all quote Newton and Brahe and Pythagoras—wait! we quote Pythagoras, too—you know what I mean—but we quote Zarathustra."

"Thus spake you," the astronomer countered, and they both laughed way too hard at this.

"Listen," challenged the astronomer, "there's no music of the spheres, no influence of the stars and the planets."

"The ones that used to be there, you mean?" the astrologer said sarcastically, and he laughed again way too hard.

"Yea, them," the astronomer scowled, feeling a pang of unemployment.

"You wanna know what I think?" the bartender chimed in.

"No," they said together and then repeated their over-the-top laugh.

"I think," the bartender offered nonetheless, "that both of you are just pissed off 'cause you're both out of a job. Here you are arguing over who does what and why, dropping names of folks I've never heard of, telling each other who's right and who's wrong, and now it doesn't matter at all. Don't get me wrong, I appreciate the place you've decided to hold these meetings, but I just wish you'd held them before there was nothing to argue about."

"You are so wrong, sir," the astrologer said. "And so serious now. You must be a Cancer."

"Used to be," the bartender leaned over to confess in a raspy confidence, and with that all three guffawed.

"Astrology," huffed the astronomer and then belched. "Like anything out there was going to have any gravitational effect on us. Did you know that this bar here has more gravitational effect on us than all of the rest of the universe combined? When it was there, that is."

"Right, when it was there," said the bartender, "which is funny, because this place has been my whole universe for twenty years."

"Mine, too, for the last month and a half," chimed in a patron at the other end of the bar. The bartender, astronomer, and astrologer raised their glasses to him.

"That's Ed," said the bartender.

"Who's Ed?" asked the astrologer.

"You won't tell me who Coperna-who or Pythagama-callit were, I'm not telling you who Ed is."

"Was," corrected Ed. "I'm not any Ed anyone used to know anymore." Ed wore dark clothes that blended in with the low-light surroundings. He wore a hoody, and he had the front of it so low over his face that it could not be seen. He could have been anybody.

The astronomer lost a bit of his buzz with Ed's downer statement, so took another swallow. "Well, Swami here is still out of a job," he taunted the astrologer. "I've still got the Moon."

"You don't have shit," the astrologer countered. "Bunch of cold, dry, dirt. You know how many courses they have at the university about your Moon. One. Moon 101. You can learn everything there is to know about the Moon in that one course. Hell, you can get a Ph.D. in Moon from taking an online course. In fact, you don't even have to take it. Hell, just pay 'em the money and they'll send you a certificate."

"Hey, I've got one of those," the bartender said.

"I've got no answer for that sorry piece of shit, the Moon," the astronomer admitted sadly. "And your astrology —"

"Which I guess really is bullshit now..." the astrologer interjected sadly.

"Thank you," agreed the astronomer, "finally!"

"They're both bullshit," concluded the bartender, topping off their mugs and pouring one for himself. The astronomer and astrologer obliged by lifting their glasses.

"Yes," admitted the astronomer, "astronomy and astrology are both bullshit. They're one and the same now. The Renaissance is officially over."

"Let's hear it for bullshit," the astrologer toasted.

"To bullshit," they all said, toasting with the hardest clinks yet of their three beers.

The bartender beamed. "There is a maturity," he said to them solemnly, a hiccup thrown in, "that comes when you've sat at this bar long enough. It is a rite of passage. It's that wisdom when you realize that all of the things that make you come to a place like this and drink them away *are* bullshit. You've arrived gentlemen," he applauded them, clapping. The other patrons, not privy to the exact reason for the clapping, joined in, welcoming the newest two members to their family.

Ed at the end of the bar arose and stumbled out of the bar. He jingled car keys as he did, but a severe man with sunglasses came out of nowhere and took them from him before he had made it completely out of the door. The man clutched Ed's elbow to lead him out, and Ed hurled a string of expletives at him worthy of a Tourette award.

"C'mon," asked the astronomer, "who's Ed?"

"Yea," chimed in the astrologer. "We won't tell anyone. Was he some kind of big shot?" The bartender leaned over the bar and motioned that they meet him halfway. He whispered.

"Used to be," he said, stealthily darting his eyes back and forth. "Ed, there, used to be the President of the United States." They all looked down in sad reverence.

"Damn," mumbled the astronomer.

"Yea," agreed the astrologer.

The astronomer and the astrologer both raised their heads back up to bar level and regarded their half-empty glasses. The bartender regarded his own half-full glass. He picked it up and raised it in toast.

"To Ed," he offered. The two other unemployed men across from him likewise lifted theirs.

"And to the new President," the astrologer toasted.

"Yea," the astronomer joined in, "whatever his name is."

The Seventh-Grader

Dear Diary,

Tonight I want to write about the stars going out. Many people think this is the worst thing that could ever happen. They sure have been acting like it was. I don't know why. Everything else seems to be the same. I miss them, too, like everyone does, but there are a lot of things more terrible than the stars going away. You could lose your dog or your rabbit could get run over by the lawnmower, which happened and that was a much worse day than when the stars went away. Or you could be a bed-wetter and everyone would see that on the Internet, but I'm not a bed-wetter. I'm just talking about someone else being a bed-wetter, like Suzy Ledbetter, which is really funny because of her name. But if Suzy saw someone was telling everyone on the Internet she wet the bed, that would be the worst thing that could happen. Much worse than the stars burning out. Almost worse than your rabbit getting run over by the lawnmower.

Believe it or not, there are even worse things than all those. One in particular I have not written about. I've been seeing Miss Terry, my therapist, who told my Mommy that I'll talk about it when I was ready. So maybe I'm ready, because I want to talk about it now, Dear Diary.

Mommy just yelled to me to see if I'm ready for bed. She makes me sleep with her, because my worst thing was when Daddy died. It was an accident, but the other man went to jail because he was being drunk and drove the wrong way. I never had a chance to say goodbye to him. My dad, I mean. I would never say goodbye to the drunk man in prison, because first of all they wouldn't let me in the prison, and second of all I hate him and wouldn't want to talk to him ever. Miss Terry says I shouldn't hate, but I should work on how I feel about him. That's hard. But I promised her I would try. But now it's just me and my Mommy, the two girls. I love her twice as much, one for her and one for when I loved my Daddy. I miss my Daddy. We both do, you know.

He would help me with chores, and one of my chores was taking care of the dogs. Feeding them, giving them a bath but not too often, and letting them out and bringing them back in. I remember once my Daddy and I were out in the backyard looking at the sky while we let the dogs do their business. It was really clear and there were a lot, I mean a lot, of stars shining and twinkling. My Daddy told me about the stars.

"The stars," he told me, "are all the good people who left us and went on to Heaven. They shine for us to remember them and to always be thankful there's a place for us to go after we die." And that was nice. Being up with the stars when we die. It was just a daddy story, but it was sweet. When you're with your dad and they tell you a daddy story, it's O.K. to believe it right then. It feels good. All those stories they tell you are love stories. That one was the last daddy story I ever heard. Mommies tell mommy stories, too, but it's always stuff like they'd rather get sick than you get sick or they'll love you forever, which you already know. Just get sick and you know what they're talking about.

After when Daddy crashed his car and died, every night when I came out to the backyard to let the dogs do their business, I looked around up there for him. For his star. I know it's silly and you can't tell which one is his, but I picked the center star of those three in a row up there. I pretended that one was his. And it maybe was. It was someone's star, right? Could just as well have been his.

And then the stars left us and went away. All those good people who left us and went to Heaven and then became stars have all left us again and went away for good. Even my Daddy. He left me. I know that they all did, I suppose, but he went along with them. And that makes me sad. Now when I look up I really feel like I don't have a dad. I've got Mom, though. But she's never been the same since Daddy went away.

At Daddy's funeral I remember she told me, "You don't know what you have until you lose it." I know what she meant. She meant she missed Daddy, like I do.

And then when the stars went away, too, including Daddy's star, and everyone in the world went crazy over it because they didn't know what they had until they all went away, she didn't go crazy over it like everyone else. She didn't have to. It didn't change her at all. She was already changed.

And now it's just her and me. The two girls. I feel just like my Mom does. All alone. With nowhere to go when I die, except six feet under the ground. That's a lonely place. Where everyone else is going one day. That's hardly a replacement for Heaven.

But I have a birthday coming up next Tuesday, so I get to miss my therapy appointment, which is good, even though I really like Miss Terry. Last time I overheard her talking to Mom about me. She told her that I might start acting out since I'm going through puberty, since I don't have a dad and all, whatever she means by acting out. But I'll finally be a teenager, so maybe I'll feel better by then. If so, then maybe my Mommy will feel better on her next birthday, too, but I doubt it.

Maybe we can act out together.

The Lovers

She had always known that they shined just for her. Everyone told her so since she was a little girl. Now that she was older and heard it less, it was no less true.

She knew the exact time and date the stars stopped shining for her. 9:30 PM.

Emily, "Emmy," knew this because it was the three-month anniversary she shared with her boyfriend on a blanket along with a bottle of wine, two Dixie cups, and a pair of binoculars. Alone with her boyfriend, with wine—so grown up. Like real adults. This was the night they had planned their sexual rite of passage and they had wanted it to be special. Even though it was a school night, that hadn't caused a problem. Each had told their parents that they were off to the library to study.

It was the night they could see the International Space Station fly over, slated for 9:17 to 9:25 PM, from north north-west to south

south-east. They had wished for a comet, but there were no comets around at the time. The ISS would have to do as the sentinel event for their consummation. It didn't hurt that there was to be a full moon, though, later in the evening. The rite of passage would be over and by the time the full moon was high enough to make shadows, they would be able to talk under it about the rest of their lives, marriage, children, the wonderful house they would have, and other romantic things.

This night and all it meant was not a casual decision. They were both virgins and it took a month of tiptoeing around the subject before the event was decided. They wanted it to be special. Paul was just as much a starry-eyed romantic as Emmy, and therefore they planned their union with the cosmos.

He had gotten the wine for them. He hadn't shaved for three days, plotting that his wisps of hair on his chin would prevent an ID check by the sales clerk. The whiskers were preposterously adolescent and the clerk knew he was too young, but sold him the wine anyway. He figured anyone who drank that garbage needed all the help he could get.

Emmy had lived by all of the Catholic rules that had been drilled into her. She truly wanted to wait until marriage for intercourse, but hormones helped her rationalize that, after all, Paul was the one she was going to marry.

Guaranteed, no doubt about it.

Boys talk about their conquests, but Paul would never do that. Boys don't respect girls who do that, but Paul would be her first and only consort, so there wouldn't be another one, ever, to wonder about her past.

There was a pesky torture, however, that resided deep in her mind, swept out of sight. It was a torment locked away in those deepest places where her deepest thoughts were. Scary thoughts. Dangerous thoughts. Things she wanted to do, like tonight, but knew she must not, because sex was something you couldn't undo.

Her sister had told her, "You can screw a light bulb and a girl, but you can't unscrew the girl." Funny at first, this clown of a phrase became the evil, grinning clown that was crying on the inside.

But love swept the pesky torture further into the recesses of the irrelevant. One moment it was there, but the next it was gone. This was love. This was Paul.

"Are you sure we should?" she asked him on the blanket, neither one of them sure about the first move.

"If not now," he asked, "when? We know it's going to be for us at some point, right?" She worried, though. She was still that light bulb, shiny and new in its shrink-wrapped package. "Besides, we have it all mapped out. We'll be able to watch the space station cross the stars, and then after that, watch the moon rise. It'll be our first moonrise *together*, if you know what I mean." He unscrewed the top of the cheap wine and poured them each a cup. "To us," he offered.

"To us," she agreed, touching her paper cup to his and then sipping. She pretended she liked it.

"Which way will it come from?" she asked.

"That way, he said, pointing toward the northwest.

"What's that star, that bright one?"

"That's the Evening Star, but it's actually Venus.

"Oh. Beautiful. Sometimes we forget to look up and see all this, huh."

"Yea, we sure do.

At precisely 9:17 PM, out of the north-northwest, a new star appeared, an upstart, a newcomer compared to the others.

"There it is," he said.

"Yea," she whispered reverently. They smiled at each other, whereupon he made the first move. With the taste of the wine still in their mouths, they kissed deeply so that they could taste the wine each offered on their lips. The wine tasted much better, this way, Emmy realized, which led to more winetasting.

By the time the ISS had passed between Ursa Minor and Ursa Major, they had their clothes off. By Perseus, he had trouble finding where he needed to go, so she helped him. By Gemini, he was finished.

They had consummated their relationship with consummate nervousness, and like the first sip of wine, she pretended she liked that, too. It all happened so fast, as first sex can. The ISS was slated to share their sky for only eight minutes, and by the time they were finished there was still a minute left in its trek across their sky toward Taurus.

But she was happy. She had finally relented to this, and she had finally defeated the guilt a good-girl upbringing had caused her. The rite was over, as well as over with, and each of them had achieved an aerobic target heart rate that night. They both lay exhausted on their backs, the blanket large enough to create a sizeable trek to any ant trying to crash their party. Besides, it was still very cool outside in central Florida, so the insect threat had yet to make such outside blanket love prohibitive. The fourth month anniversary, Emmy figured, would be pushing their luck at striving for such coexistence with the world's biting, stinging, and sucking creatures. A second blanket, folded, offered her dignity in the aftermath, and he unfolded it to cover them both.

"That was nice," she told him.

"Yea, it was," he agreed. "I love you, Emmy," he added, contracting the wonderful, gushing, exhilarating mental illness of deceptive love that comes with first sex. She snuggled closer to him again, just as infected.

"Me, too, Paul," she said back to him.

Now they revisited the astronautic celebration that would solidify the memory.

"Look! Quick, it's almost gone," Paul said excitedly, and he raised his arm straight into the air, a lone index finger pointing, tracking, and slowly moving south south-east for the last of the man-made star's graceful arc across their very own sky. They were lucky enough to have a clear, dark night due to the moon not rising until 9:30. "Here," he offered, "take a look."

She quickly grabbed the binoculars he offered, but the angle of view was too narrow to find it, so she went by naked eyesight again, successfully re-following her boyfriend's finger to the point of light. Only seconds later, the ISS was gone. They sat up again to pour their wine.

"It's gone," she pouted.

"It was only up there for a few minutes."

"But we missed most of it," she complained.

"I didn't miss anything," Paul said, smiling, cupping her face in his hands.

"Me, either," she smiled back.

"We ought to buy a star for this night," she blurted excitedly. "From one of those places that give out deeds to the stars."

"Yea, that'd be cool."

"And every time we looked up and saw that star, we could think of us together, on the blanket, this night, and…everything."

"Yea." He took out his cellphone and did a search for star registries. "Here, Star Conveyances and Registration International."

"Lemme see!" she said, snatching the phone from him. "Oh, let's do it Paul." She handed it back to him.

"Sure. What star?" he asked. She looked toward where the ISS had first appeared.

"What's that one?" she asked, pointing to the end of the Little Dipper. He opened his planetarium app that was illuminated in only red graphics and fonts and identified the one she indicated.

"Polaris," he said. "The North Star." He switched back to the Star Conveyances website. "$150," he said. "I can afford that."

"No, we'll both buy it. We'll share it. It will be a symbol of what you can have when you're in love." She laughed with enthusiasm. "Go ahead, pay for it. I'll pay my half to you tomorrow." He used some finger swipes and made the purchase.

"It's ours," he announced proudly.

"What else can you see with those?" she asked, pointing to the binoculars.

"Andromeda?" Paul asked.

"What?" Emmy asked back.

"Do you want to see it?"

"Sure. What is it? A star, constellation, what?"

"A whole 'nother galaxy," he replied.

"Guess we can't buy that. Yea, I do want to see that," she said. "We can name our baby Andromeda if I'm pregnant.

Pregnant? he thought. *Ridiculous*. Pregnancy had as much to do with tonight, he thought, as leprechauns or unicorns.

"Well, we better hurry if we wanna see it," he warned. "Moon's rising in a minute or so." He turned on his smartphone and launched his planetarium app again. When he turned it off, he lay back down next to her and quietly observed, darting his eyes back and forth. Finally, he lifted up the binoculars and honed in on the fuzzy object.

He handed the binoculars to Emmy and whispered, as if whispering would keep the visual trajectory he had discovered stable. "Look," he said, almost imperceptibly. "Follow my finger, then look through the lenses."

"I don't see it," she said. She let the binoculars wander until Paul put his hand on hers to stop their jittery, frantic search.

"Little biddy movements," he instructed. Finally she saw a blurry object that feebly shined at a magnitude 3.44 that night.

"Another galaxy?" she asked.

"Yes."

"How big?"

"Bigger than ours," he answered. "Bigger than the Milky Way."

"Wow," she murmured. Without moving the binoculars, she wondered out loud. "I wonder how many couples, you know—like us, are on a world there, in a field, under a blanket, you know—like us, looking at our Milky Way the way we're looking at them."

"Well, it's got a trillion stars."

"So, likely?" she asked.

"I would think guaranteed," he said softly.

"It's nice to think we're looking at each other," she said. "Like all four of us are in love and we're all connected across the light years to each other."

"The power of love," he said, and then he leaned over to kiss her cheek, which moved her gaze ever so slightly. "Oh," she blurted, annoyed, "you made me lose it. You made it disappear."

"Keep looking," he insisted. "You'll get it right back."

"I am. Nothing. Is the Moon out yet?"

"Just a faint glow to the east so far."

"Still nothing," she reported with disappointment and frustration. She took the binoculars away from her eyes and looked at the patch of sky where she had aimed them. "They're all gone," she told Paul, who was not looking at anything but her.

"What?" he whispered into her ear.

"Look," she said loudly. He turned away and then bolted up.

"Did it get overcast all of a sudden?" he asked.

"The bright Moon?" she offered.

"No, not even over the horizon yet." He took the binoculars again. "Nothing. Like they've all gone out," he reported. Emmy flinched.

"Well," she said, "we know that didn't happen. But it sure looks like it." Her attitude had changed. It was as if she had taken everything personally.

"I don't get it," he said, perplexed. "Nothing to see up there. Everything's gone." He looked around in all directions. "No clouds. I don't think there are any. What the hell! Look! Even Venus is gone over there."

"And our star, too," she cried. "That whole galaxy just turned off like a light bulb." She paused. "Like someone just unscrewed it."

"There's got to be a reason, an explanation. Probably a high fog blew in. Gotta be, right? I mean, gotta be…right?"

"You figure it out. I already have." She felt years of Sunday school guilt come over her. Her tone was quarrelsome, and he caught the change.

"What's wrong?" he asked. She sat upright, then without explanation began to put her clothes back on. She still had half a cup of wine sitting on the blanket. She picked it up and threw the cup onto the adjacent grass. "What's wrong, Emmy?" he asked again.

"Everything," she answered, and what she felt should have been obvious to him he had completely missed. Gone with the stars.

Men were from Mars, which no longer existed, and women were from Venus, which no longer existed, and their star, Polaris, their stellar embodiment, no longer existed. Here on Earth, which still did, their closeness separated faster and more vastly than the original inflation of space-time after the first 10^{-36} second of the Big Bang.

"Better to have loved and lost than to never have loved at all," Paul might say.

"Not really," Emmy would say.

On the night of their rite of passage, the ISS had undergone its own rite of passage—a passage through a starless sky. But it would not be Emmy's and Paul's sky anymore, for they never again would nurture their feelings under it.

And the stars never again would be above the ISS, sealing its own doom.

The Balladeer

We've let the fire go out and the burning epoch ends here;
Our long incend'ry journey from caves succumbed this year.
Prometheus will keep his liver but Man will spill his bile,
For the stars have flickered out and hope's gone out of style.

My true love is silent, her voice left with the stars;
Our ties together have reversed, because effect now looks for
cause.
Our unborn children will live in a world roofed in decay;
They will never know a horoscope but live uncertain ev'ry day.

Our broken hearts are manifest, we feel so terribly alone;
Our hollow souls have already left us, forced in vain to roam.
Our future's certain by now, there's nothing for us there;
So there's nothing for us here, nothing left to dare.

The Stock Broker

Capitalism gave everyone a wake-up call.

For all of the sociological upheaval that sudden isolation created, it was the day-to-day goings-on that re-established the status-quo, albeit with an unidentifiable sadness and hopelessness that everyone had to deal with on their own terms.

Those who had given up and stopped functioning in their days-to-days found that interest cruelly accrued on the late mortgage payments that were not made. People discovered that they still couldn't eat without paying for their food, even in a world of cosmic implications. Tuition was still due. The fiscal enforcement by the people who had plans trickled down to those who had given up on their plans because of a starless sky. Ultimately those mired into inactivity because of unanswered love for the stars began to resume their plans. There was no choice. The homeless numbers had risen, but within sixteen months they had leveled off back to the starry-skied levels. The GNP of the world's Big 8 stumbled, but was back on track within eighteen months.

The suicide rate tripled worldwide, and it would not level back off again until the first generation of starless children assumed the largest age demographic some twenty years later. The day after the stars went out, Wall Street crashed. Nearly eleven trillion dollars of the NYSE disappeared before noon, at which time the President ordered the exchange closed. That evening, when he addressed the nation and the world, he set in motion a rekindling of the market, and within two days it had recovered over 60% of its losses. It was the biggest pendulum swing in stocks ever recorded.

Kenny Heigle was bitterly disappointed that he was part of the big sellout, along with the other lemmings, before the President rescued the market. Everyone he knew had cashed out along with him. With regrettable hindsight acuity, he was even more disappointed he hadn't bought low the day of the crash, even though under any other circumstances he would have been tempted to do just that. What stopped him was a certainty that nothing would ever recover. It seemed written in the stars. It would have been throwing good money after bad.

Many speculators did buy very low at the opportunity, and they became wealthy when the market stabilized upward again. But not Kenny. He had missed his chance, caught in a trance of inactivity like most of the world the day after. His was the only telescope sale online for the month, and he bought it to watch for any universal burps that might set the pendulum in swing once more. He would not miss another chance to buy low. The market had reset to a begrudged correction, however, and so he had to wait.

His was one of the last American families to continue the tradition of family supper every evening. It became difficult for his wife to pull it off, because she was forced to replace the large weekly shopping runs with daily as-needed piecemeal visits to the grocery. The larger debits were no longer feasible on their income, credit had been maxed out, and now even the cash transactions were iffy. Steaks became chicken. Chicken became beans. His wife, Patty, remained as best she could dutiful to her domestic obligations, usually having dinner ready by the time Kenny got home.

This particular day had been difficult for her.

"Thirty-two dollars and twenty-two cents," the cashier had said. Patty looked into her purse and saw the solitary twenty. She knew the outcome, but played the game anyway. She handed the cashier the twenty, then she unzipped a coin compartment and fished out exact change. The cashier looked at her, not judging, not pitying, but just expectantly. She was an older woman.

Probably a cashier her whole life, Patty thought to herself. *I used to drive a Mercedes. Do you even have a car?*

Reckoning struck.

"Do you have a ten?" the cashier asked, whereupon Patty went through the motions of rifling through her purse. Of course she would have a ten. Somewhere.

An emaciated woman behind her patted her pug. The dog was wrapped in a colorful blanket in the child seat of her basket, which otherwise had Ensure and many packs of Little Caesar dog food.

"Honey, here," the woman said to Patty. Patty turned around. The woman had a ten-dollar bill in her hand. She was offering it to her. She was proffering charity. Patty's face went red with embarrassment.

"Oh, no, I couldn't, really."

"No, go ahead, take it." The woman leaned across her small dog. "Excuse me, Elvis," she said to him. She whispered, "I'm not long for this world. And I'm not taking this Hamilton with me. So go ahead."

"I'm sorry," Patty said, "and I don't want to appear ungrateful or rude, but I really don't need the charity."

"Tell you what, honey, since you know your ten's in there somewhere...Us girls, right? With our purses...since it's there—we all know it is—just take the ten now and we can go outside and dump out that crazy purse of yours and you can give it right back to me."

"So what's next?" Patty asked Kenny, as they prepared to eat the rest of their cash and some of someone else's. Their two children, 16-year-old Kayla and 13-year-old Tyler, were silent, knowing where this conversation was going. They had gone from Mercedes' and BMWs to a single Ford something-or-other model. They had downsized to an apartment, paying rent to someone who wasn't as successful as Kenny had been in the day. Life went from sweet to a struggle.

"What's next," Kenny answered, somewhat persnickety, "is we wait for the market to come back."

"When the stars come back, right?" Patty chided him.

"It's the age old formula, Patty. Buy low, sell high."

"But you sold low," she reminded him, as she did daily.

"Everyone did. What was I supposed to do? The stars go away and the market crashes. Lower and lower. I had to jump out, had to unload so we'd have something. We've been through this over and over. What makes you think my strategy has changed."

"But now you're buying again, and the market's not any better. Some strategy."

"Buying low, Patty, buying low."

"O.K., so you've cashed out everything to keep buying low. We don't own our home, we don't own our car, and we don't even own a reputation anymore. You should have seen me at the grocery today." She was on the verge of angry tears.

"The stars will come back, Dad," said Tyler. Kenny smiled at him; Patty tossed her head away from them with a huff of disgust.

"Brent says we're gonna do fine," Kayla chimed in.

"Brent?" laughed Tyler. "Kooky Brent?"

"Brent knows a lot," Kayla objected.

"Does he know when the stars are coming back?" Tyler asked, and laughed again. "Does he know when his dad's coming back?"

"What if they don't come back?" Patty asked her husband, not expecting an answer.

"Maybe we should ask Brent," Tyler struck again. "If he knows about the stars, maybe he knows when his dad's coming back, too?" Kayla burst out crying and ran from her chair, up the stairs, into her room, her journey ending with a splintering slam of a door.

"Tyler," Patty said to her son. "Have some compassion. My goodness! A lot of people killed themselves with everything that's happened. It's the children who suffer."

"Yea, a lot did. After they sold low," Kenny added. "Some people just didn't have the guts, I guess." Patty shot him a disgusted look. "But Ty, please, you know how sensitive your sister is about Brent."

"Just because Brent's dad killed himself doesn't mean we need to watch everything we say," Tyler complained.

"Tyler!" Patty scolded him. "Compassion? Please? If Brent hurts, your sister hurts. What's happening to you? What you did was a little cruel, don't you think?"

"You want to know what I think?" Tyler asked curtly.

"Oh, boy," Kenny said, rolling his eyes.

"I think I'm sick of all this stars crap," he began. "I think it's about time everyone grow up and stop running around like chickens with their heads cut off. Everyone should just shut up about it and start living. Dad, you're waiting for stars to come back so you can invest according to some strategy that we don't understand. Mom, you need to stop complaining and deal with our financial situation. Dad's smart and—"

"Not about this mysterious strategy," Patty interjected.

"O.K., not about that strategy."

"Hey!" Kenny objected.

"But he'll come through," Tyler continued. "And if it gets harder before it gets better, then tough shit!"

"Tyler!" Patty scolded him again.

"Watch that mouth, Tyler," Kenny said to his son.

"And if it takes a while to get better, then we have each other, right?" Tyler said, resetting the conversation. "We love each other, right?"

"Including Kayla?" Kenny asked.

"I'm not joking. Of course, Kayla, too. So everyone needs to get off their asses and live according to the world the way it is now. Dad, if you keep pining for the stars to come back, you gonna keep being sort of a loser. Mom, if you keep bitchin' at Dad, you're gonna lose him. And me, too. Can everyone just shut the fuck up and get back to normal?"

Tyler rested his case, taking a mouthful from the glass of his Coke he had spiked with Jack Daniels. His parents were agape, as if in self-caricature of their shock. He put the glass down and looked at them calmly. "So," he said, putting his hands together, "what are your thoughts?" There was a pregnant pause—a troubled pregnancy's pause.

"Go to your room!" Patty and Kenny said together.

"No," answered Tyler.

The Terminal Patient

It seemed that dying was not such a dreadful thing anymore, now that the stars were gone. She had no more living family. No children. Not even an ex. She had no stars or planets or friends.

She had a dog and in some respects had a cat, too.

Anna could see herself going out with the stars. It lent a romantic respite from the toxic melancholy that had carried with her since she had heard her diagnosis. Among her phases of denial, anger, pleading, and acceptance, romance snuck in right at the end, courtesy of absentee heavenly bodies that had led the way. *Yes, I can go out with the stars*, she mused. When she ate, drank, slept, and breathed her disease and mortality every waking and sleeping moment since her bad news, it was easy, even comforting, to imagine that the disappearance of the stars had a fateful relationship with her own pending disappearance.

Let the world do without the both of us, she thought. *Then they'll see.* A small black Pug, the only friend she had, jumped onto her lap.

"I won't leave you," she promised the small dog. "No, we're a package deal, huh?" The Pug who barked his responses. "I should have named you Astro, right, Elvis?" she said to Elvis, what she had really named him. "Or Krypto or even…Major Tom! Yes!" Elvis yipped in agreement to the happy chirping sounds of her voice. "So, what do you think about all this missing stars nonsense? Do you even know what stars are? I guess not, sweetie." She made exaggerated smooching noises all around his head as Elvis licked her all over her face.

"I guess I should feel deserted," she said to him. "My life is leaving me and now my stars have left me." Elvis jammed his snout into her belly firmly and snorted and sniffed rapidly. He could smell her disease. He had smelled it long before any biopsies, scans, or even suspicions had hinted of it. "But I'm not leaving you, no way. Not you. I would never do that, would I?"

She knew that to Elvis, she was his sky, his ultimate destination, his million points of light. She was his hopes and dreams and when his time came, she would even be his own eternal rest, because dogs were not supposed to outlive their masters. He had never even seen the stars because he had never looked any higher than her face. He had never heard the music she played, because he never listened any further than her voice. Just as Man had reached for the stars, Elvis had reached for her. Her voice was the only music he could ever hear. It might just as well have been the music of the spheres, for she was the radius of his own small sphere. His small canine brain saw himself as much a part of her as her own arms and legs and tumor. When she suffered, he suffered. When she would grab her lower abdomen and groan in pain, Elvis would slink toward her, his legs double-jointed and his tail down. It did not matter to Elvis that the stars were gone; it only mattered to him that Anna was still here. But as small as his mind was, it sensed her coming departure from his world. She thought of it often, too, but she never spoke of it to him. She knew some things dogs understood without knowing any words except for *treat, vet, bath* or his name. Anna was fond of saying that dogs were a gift from God, and truly their dedication – total, loving, even ridiculous – could only have come from God.

As special as the stars themselves.

She also had a cat that she seldom saw. It was an outside cat, living a feral feline life that was interrupted only for a visit to the milk bowl on her step. She knew that the cat knew there were no more stars but that it simply didn't care. She knew that cats know almost everything but don't care about almost all of it. They were survivors and would do just fine dealing with this loss. But she also knew a cat would have no clue of the rot inside her that doomed her and threatened the milk supply.

Elvis knew that no dog should outlive his master. That's just the way it was. It was *the law*. His small canine mind couldn't use a vocabulary to put it into words, but somewhere among his simple synapses he could sense the train wreck coming and that his stars, his ultimate destination, and his million points of light would soon be gone. He couldn't reconcile this with *the law*, which made him cry at night, even if Anna didn't know why.

He cried for her. He cried at night, even if Anna didn't know why. He cried for both of them, even if Anna didn't know how.

She labeled Elvis her comfort dog, insisting he accompany her to the grocery, to the mall, and heaven help the unfortunate complainer who disapproved. He even went with her to her doctor's office for the weekly bloodwork and downhill assessments, courtesy of old, persnickety Dr. Burgess. Her kindly companion mostly succeeded in his role, comforting her in everything but the little daggers of abdominal pain that seemed to be coming more frequently. That would be too much to ask, for it was an ugly pain with which no comfort animal should have any dealings whatsoever.

Old Dr. Burgess's office was vinyl flooring with years of wax layers piled into a hazy topsoil of trapped medicinal molecules that had floated down over time and gotten stuck, awaiting shuffling feet to rekindle. She smelled them all as she walked through the long hallway, parting an isopropyl Red Sea of suspended aromatics. Elvis sneezed.

"Oh, God bless his little heart," Anna said to the dog.

It was a long, dark hallway speckled with doors that she half-expected to begin opening and slamming shut in a theatre cliché from the door-slamming school of British farce. The fluorescents mostly behaved themselves, except for the one that flickered and buzzed. She knew right where to go, and at the end of the veneered hall she opened his door, sat in her usual chair and settled in, waiting for him to acknowledge her from across his messy desk. He looked up from the chart—her chart—and began the visit with his look of disapproval for the dog on her lap. "Don't even start. He's my comfort animal."

"Comfort, hmmm…You shouldn't have canceled your chemotherapy appointments or refused your radiation if you wanted comfort. In fact, you have refused to discuss further any remedies at all."

"Remedies? Is that what those things are? They're remedies? They will fix me?"

"Anna, you know what I mean. I agree that the survival rate—"

"My rate? I'm going to have a rate? Of survival? A rate of remedy. How fast are your remedies?" Elvis picked up on the sarcasm and yipped a high-pitched bark that hurt Dr. Burgess' ears. He flinched.

"Ow! Enough to make you deaf!" he grumbled.

"Deaf-*er*, you mean. 'cause you're not listening."

"No reconsideration on the chemo, Anna?" She only sighed. "Anna?" he repeated.

"No, not for me."

"Why do you keep refusing?" he asked.

"Again, you ask me? Again, Dr. B., I ask you back, have you seen the night sky?"

"Oh, that. Yes, I have. And again *I* ask, how does that figure into a decision to refuse what's best for you?"

"Dr. B., I've had radiation all my life. Cosmic rays, X-rays, gamma rays, microwaves, ocean waves, death rays—all from the stars."

"Ocean waves come from the Moon."

"Same thing, smarty-pants. And the day they left is the day you gave me my diagnosis. Advanced this, advanced that."

"Advanced mixed muellerian carcinosarcoma."

"If you say so."

"Well, then," he said with a mischievous smile, "maybe all that radiation kept your cancer away. More reason to consider it now since you're on your own without them."

"Funny, Doc, real funny," she said. "A 10% survival rate with your man-made radiation?"

"Yea, I know."

He understood. She knew he understood.

"You have to try," he urged her, having to try.

"No, I really don't. Look, all I know is that I came from dust and to dust I will return. With or without radiation."

"You came from the dust of stars," Dr. Burgess added. "Stardust to stardust."

"Pardon?" she said, a little confused.

"We all came from the stars. The first stars had hydrogen, then helium. Then they exploded, and they threw out the heavier atoms that were made with all these forces. Then those clumped together and became stars again; then *they* exploded, throwing out heavier stuff. This is all stuff that made our Sun and Earth, you and me." He sneered at Elvis. "*Him*, too."

"Sick 'im, Elvis," she joked, but Elvis didn't know what that meant. She sat quietly, considering this tale of creation and renewals. Finally, realizing this gave no comfort, she said, "And with the stars gone, then that means you and I and all the rest of everything on this Earth are the last pieces of star stuff there will ever be."

Now Dr. Burgess sat quietly, because that was quite a sentiment. "Well," he finally said, "except for the Sun."

"How long before that goes away?"

"Hopefully, not for five billion years or so."

"Five billion?"

"Or sooner. Nothing would surprise me anymore."

"No matter when, Dr. B., I'll be long gone before that."

Anna's doctor wondered if there was some genetic memory in her DNA from the previous stars which had collapsed and exploded violently enough to make the iron that sat in her hemoglobin, even though she was anemic; the oxygen she breathed, even though she was short of breath; the stuff that made the bacteria—both the good and the bad, although in her body the bad seemed to be overpowering the good. The hydrogen, the nitrogen, the magnesium, the sodium, the potassium—all of these things that had been part of the progenitor stars that eventually had made possible her life—he wondered if there were wisps of blueprints her DNA harbored which could, albeit on a molecular level, spin tales of the stars gone.

"I stand corrected," she said, breaking his reverie. "Not dust to dust or stardust to stardust. My dust—my dust is supposed to go back into the stars, but I guess that's impossible now. My dust will be wasted."

"Don't throw it away just yet, Anna. It's good dust."

"Shame," she said. She began to rise from the chair and Elvis jumped down. She left with Elvis prancing behind her. To a dog, life was good.

There weren't many days left for her — for them — but during the few they shared, Anna and Elvis were happy. Even when Anna was more sarcoma than she was Anna. No dog should outlive his master, Elvis kept gestalting in his limited dog brain way, without words. So when Anna finally left Elvis' world, he felt very un-dogly about himself. She wasn't supposed to leave him first.

No dogs should outlive their masters. She had broken *the law.*

There was a celebration of life at Anna's house the evening of the funeral. Dr. Burgess was there. The pastor who presided over the burial was there, too. It wasn't important to Elvis that there was no one else present, because dogs do not keep score, even for what are supposed to be celebrations. The two celebrants only counted to two, but he had an equation with no sum.

He left the kitchen through the doggy door and walked into the backyard. The feral cat hissed at him, but he didn't care. He saw her on the fence, and she seemed stunned that he didn't care. His eyes didn't stop there. He continued to look up, beyond Anna-height for the first time. He reached a point where he might see the twinkling, sparkly dots of light strewn across the sky that everyone was grieving over. There were none. He listened for the music of the spheres. There was none.

He wondered just what all the fuss was about, compared to his Anna being gone.

The Zoologist

Warblers had been his life since undergraduate school. His thesis was about Warblers. He had met his wife while studying Warblers. He thought about Warblers more than he thought about his grown children. Warblers were wonderful, from their spring molt transformation into the bold yellows, sooty grays, and bright whites to their unique chirps.

But Warblers' migrating habits depended on starlight by which to navigate, and now they were confused. They were dying, and he estimated they had about three more years before they would be extinct.

He and his entomology friends compared notes. Many insects also were behaving oddly since the stars had disappeared. Crickets began using only their left or their right legs to chirp their turf and mating calls, instead of both. This made country living a bit quieter, but the night more than made up for it with the arrival of the "barking" of nocturnal spiders everywhere. Arachnologists quickly described the mechanism that made this noise, and it just added a footnote to a creature that had not changed in any other perceivable way.

Cockroaches became disagreeable, though, even hostile and aggressive. They were non grata to begin with, but when they were reported to frequently swarm babies' cribs, ecological prohibitions on many insecticides were rescinded. People hated cockroaches before this, but now the cockroaches seemed to hate people right back.

The stars and the crickets, the spiders, and the cockroaches— who knew?

But Warblers Dr. Congeni knew about. In fact, they were the first thing he thought about the morning after the stars went out. Warblers liked to eat cockroaches, so there was that added injury to the ecosystem he fretted over.

His position at the university aviary became much more important that morning, because the Warblers were the only species that relied so heavily on the stars, notwithstanding the sudden epiphany of barking spiders, half-hearted cricket wooers, and hateful cockroaches. Everyone with a fondness for birds—or even sensitivity for the permanence and heartbreak of extinction—asked him for a solution. But the stars were as much a part of the ecosystem as the Warblers eating the bugs that barked or that swarmed hatefully. It was a beautiful relationship originating from the cold and vacuum of space: photons had still found their way to rescue Warblers, guiding them to flock to wherever they had to go in North America.

Until the night the stars went out.

Now the birds went nowhere, hunkering down by the millions in southern Arizona and New Mexico. Good news for all the cats there.

Dr. Congeni was invited to make a pilgrimage to the US-Mexico border to study the Warbler non-migration phenomenon but declined. He knew the Warblers wouldn't be telling him anything. They didn't need him. They needed the stars and the stars were gone. He might as well have dedicated his life to a species of dinosaur. Nevertheless, the world of aviary zoology continued to relentlessly besiege him via email, phone calls, and even unannounced visits from interested parties like the one he noticed standing at his office door. The woman had seen it open and had walked in tenuously just a step. She held in her hand the textbook on flocking behaviors in which he had authored the chapter on Warblers.

"It's alright, please come in."

He was a friendly sort, showing in his tone and on his face. He wore a natural smile. She pulled a chair from the corner of his office and placed it across from him.

"May I?" she asked.

"Certainly," he answered. He was at his desk, leaning back in that way mothers always warn and fuss about.

"You can break your neck doing that," she said with mock maternal severity. He fell forward landing the front legs of his chair firmly on the floor.

"Do you know the leading cause of broken necks?" he asked her, still smiling politely.

"Leaning back on your chair?"

"No, actually, its auto accidents. I don't think chair-leaning even registers on the pie chart." She laughed. He returned the good humor by sticking out his hand. "Jay Congeni," he offered.

"Pleased to meet you, Dr. —"

"Call me Jay, please."

"Pleased to meet you, Jay," she said taking his hand. His hands were perfect, she noticed. "I'm Tess McKnight."

"I've always thought that was a beautiful name, Tess. What can I do for you?" he asked her. She held out the textbook.

"First things first, could you please autograph this?"

"I only wrote a chapter," he said, taking it from her contritely.

"Oh, but what a chapter," she gushed. "If you read your chapter first and then read all the others, you realize that they all just repeat everything you say in yours. Just not as well."

He opened the book to its table of contents. Over the chapter heading that read, "North America: the Yellow-rumped Warbler's Continent, by Dr. Jay Congeni," he wrote with a cheap Bic pen: *To Tess, best wishes*. He closed it so quickly that there would be a shroud-like backwards imprint of it on the opposing page. He handed it back to her.

"I know this isn't the only reason you came."

"No, it isn't," she admitted. "I came to discuss a possibility with you."

"O.K., sure," he said.

"Well, the stars are gone and the Warblers are fucked." He was noticeably taken aback. "Oh, I'm sorry, so sorry, that just sort of came out."

"No, no, Tess, it's quite alright. I've certainly heard that word before. In fact," he said in a hushed tone, "I've even used it before." Tess giggled. She was a very pretty woman, and pretty women can get away with more.

"Do they have any hope?" she asked.

"I'm afraid not."

"I came here to bounce an idea off of you." Dr. Congeni sat up straight. He seemed interested. "How many planes to you think are in the air at any time?" she asked.

He thought about it and finally answered, "Oh, I don't have a clue. I suppose about a thousand all over the world."

"How 'bout seven?"

"Seven thousand? My goodness, I had no idea."

"So, what if—and I'm just throwing this out—what if they were to be synchronized at night in a way that would mimic the stars going east to west?"

"Intriguing," he mumbled. "What about people who want to go west to east? Or North to South?"

"They can do that during the daytime. I'd imagine it would simplify air traffic control a bit, all the planes going in the same direction all the time."

"How would you go about getting that considered? You've got hundreds of airline companies, thousands of airports, a lot of capitalism in the way, special interests..."

"That's where you come in."

"Me?"

"Yes. No one may care about the Warbler—oh, I didn't mean how that sounded—you know what I mean. However—and that's however with a capital H—people do care about crazy swarming insects, hostile cockroaches, and extinction and any unlinking of links in the ecosystem. You could make a case for it with the Warbler as the poster child for helping the environment. Everything would benefit."

"You're not here just for you, are you?"

"No, Jay, I'm not."

"And you're not here for the Warblers, right?"

"Right."

"So who? Who sent you?"

"I'm the sole proprietor of Star Conveyances and Registration International."

"The Star Registry?"

"Star Conveyances and Registration International sells certificates that assign stars to people. It's a romantic notion, actually. Of course, no one owns the stars."

"Not any more, certainly."

"Right." She paused to redirect the conversation back on topic. "We could offer to redesign commercial air flight itineraries that could be the stars every night."

"Not for just the Warblers, then."

"No—I mean, yes, they would benefit. But Star Conveyances and Registration International could get back to their important work of registering those pining for the good ol' days."

"So, really, Tess, this is really just for your company."

"Yes, us too, I admit. But like I said, everything would benefit. But we need a jumpstart. One that is noble, altruistic, and can be sold as important to Mother Earth."

"Sold?"

"I didn't mean the vulgar meaning of 'sold.' Jay, I'm here just to say that everyone could benefit. Migratory birds, the food chain from the insects to hibernating bears, and surely Man himself."

"And the Star Registry."

"Yes, and Star Conveyances and Registration International, too. Is that so bad? There's really no downside, is there?"

"Even if I were to agree to participate in this sham, Tess—"

"Oh, please, Jay, don't be like that."

"Even if I were to agree to it, there's the uphill commercial battle to get the airlines, the TSA, the avionics industry, and the FAA to agree to it."

"They don't have to."

"Oh?"

"No. If they say no, and they probably will, at least the subject's been burned onto the environmentally sensitive conscience of everyone who watches the media. Because of its ecological sentiment, a grassroots swelling of support will begin, no doubt. And we make the Star Registry non-profit, just to prove to everyone our sincerity.

"And when the airlines say no—you said they probably would, where does that leave you?"

"With all the publicity, the notoriety of being denied—victimized, actually—by the profiteers at the airlines. Then we crowdfund a new company that will launch a small series of highly reflective satellites into low orbit, each slightly faster than geostationary, and create our own nighttime planetarium. East to west, following the terminator around the Earth. Who needs the stars? We can make our own." She smiled. "And who needs the damn airlines, right?"

Dr. Congeni sat still and thought for a moment. He was no longer wearing his default smile.

"I'm sorry, Tess, but this all sounds really crazy."

"I'm sorry you feel that way, Jay. Imagine a corporation that can re-establish migratory patterns."

"Or control them?"

"Well, in the wrong hands. That's why it must be Star Conveyances and Registration International. No one loves the stars more than us. All we want to do is replace what we had before. And while we're at it, your Warblers get their nightlights. No one—I mean no one—will complain about giving the world back its stars. There's a lucrative opportunity for those who can control the paths of the stars. Commercial opportunities." She put her hands on his desk and leaned toward him. "You could be issued preferred stock as an incentive, you know. You would own a piece of it. You don't exactly have a golden parachute at this place."

Dr. Congeni watched with some amount of disgust as she pulled herself back against her seat back and remained silent for a moment to allow him to consider. Did everything have a commercial aspect, he wondered? Is there profit to be made with every opportunity—even tragedy? It really was vulgar, this selling of the idea. And it introduced into a silly company a dynamic it never dreamed of having before—power.

"Well," Tess asked, "what do you think?"

"I think you should leave."

Now it was her turn to be taken aback. She glared at him for a moment and then she slid the autographed book toward him on his desktop.

"Fuck your goddamn Warblers," she said with hostility. She rose from her chair and straightened out her jacket smartly by tugging it down in one stroke and then buttoned it. All the time she looked him right in the eye. She turned around and began to walk out of his office forever.

"Oh, and Tess?" he called to her.

She spun around just as smartly. "Yes, Dr. Congeni?"

"How much do you think that preferred stock would be worth?"

The Have-nauts

The International Space Station now sported elbows and wings and warts of nearly twenty nations, afloat a gravity wave that kept it falling forward on that thin line between smashing into or forever escaping its planet. The ISS, now one of only four remaining celestial bodies in the universe, boarded forty astronauts, cosmonauts, takinauts, and other xenonauts who sat resentfully on vacation, their orders suspended until further notice.

"Idleness is the devil's playground," said Astronaut Parks, his Texan drawl making it take twice as long to say.

"We read you, Captain Parks," came the reply from Houston. "Please stand by."

"As we have," Captain Parks repeated again this morning, like the previous mornings. Standing by now meant until tomorrow and meant a word-for-word repeat of the same conversation.

Captain Parks had been the first person to observe the sudden absence of the stars, and the rest of the ISS occupants were the most frightened of all humans who had witnessed this sea change of astronomy. The disappearance of the annoying cosmic ray flashes in their aqueous humor wasn't much of a trade-off when they realized that it was because there were no longer any rays, cosmic or otherwise.

Captain Parks' doctoral thesis had been on Cepheid Variables, by which the universe's age and distances were determined. Now there were no variables out there, no variation. Their Sun was still steady, but besides that there were just Earth and that extra rock, the Moon. And them.

His scientific counterpart, Dr. Alan Thiel, an ecologist, had done his thesis on the doomed reliance on colonization to allow the Earth's people to escape the soiling of their planet, an extinction event, or even a catastrophe of their Sun. Based on his thesis, he and a collaborator, Dr. Cydney Haas, had written a New York Times bestseller that delighted the environmental movement by stating the case that relying on colonization was an empty promise and we could never accomplish it. This was tantamount to announcing there had better evolve a better plan for preserving the world we have, for we had nowhere to run. Dr. Thiel cited technological barriers, religious intolerance, economic roadblocks, and political realities. The book had made it very difficult for him to end up on the ISS, yet, here he was, investigating an empty sky, a final barrier which spoke loud and clear: forget theories, theses, counterarguments, and manifest destiny; there really was no place to go now and no one to push out of the way. One night, in the twinkling of an eye, he had been vindicated.

Brian Parks was an Air Force pilot and a veteran of a Space Shuttle mission in the nineties. Dr. Thiel was the only other American there, and both had been prepared to receive three more Americans in exchange for their return home on the Soyuz.

All of that was put on hold, which Capt. Parks and Dr. Thiel could not understand, because it was a metaphysical hold. Nothing had really changed except a lot of philosophy.

And civil order and religious affiliations, both of these for the worse.

Day after day they all stood by. After 120 days of standing by, the other nations' spacefarers on board the ISS were keen to Dr. Thiel's idea to have a multinational meeting on board. Its purpose was to establish a position that they could propose to their respective nations together. It was hoped that such a unified approach would get the governments' attention in the matter, since they were now on a 30-day countdown for running out of food. The Russian oxygen generator, inert, had needed the replacement parts on the astronaut exchange that was to see the Americans home. Now all on board were relying on the pressurized tanks, but even they had a low-amount alarm due to go off in 45 days.

Certainly, everyone agreed, they won't just let us all die up here. But certainly, everyone also agreed, it didn't look like anyone down there would do anything until they had to.

All of the inhabitants were confused as to the little or no interaction from below, and so they were all present and participatory at the meeting, held in the "Big Tube," the long, large cylinder that had been installed the previous year. It had been meant to be used for medical experiments that required some amount of distance, and it was a welded 2-piece construction which was 20 feet in diameter and 100 feet long. All 40 were in attendance, each floating gently but tethered by a holding strap to one hand.

"I'd like to call this meeting to order," Dr. Thiel announced. "Let it be recorded that members of the following nations are present: United States of America, Russia, People's Republic of

China, the United Kingdom, Canada, Germany, France, Italy, Spain, South Africa, Pakistan, Japan, and India.

"I have called this meeting so that we could present our position and concerns with one voice. While politicos philosophize down below, we have become a minor concern. They've put more funding into Hubble and Webb than into our ISS here, all in the hopes of finding the faintest sparkle out there. I find this ironic, because aside from the Sun and the Moon, we're the brightest object in the sky right now. While they posture themselves to deal at the international, national, regional, and even neighborhood levels so that they can navigate the by-products and side effects of this missing sky problem, we risk all of the consequences of neglect. When a lot of money is being gobbled up in phantom jaws, there is none for us."

"I make a motion," offered Leonid Restov, the Russian biologist, "that we form a committee to draft our requests and needs and to emphasize a timeline."

"We're the committee," Capt. Parks said angrily, and after a moment of murmuring, Dr. Restov withdrew his motion.

"Right," agreed Dr. Chun, who wondered if his nation would be upset with him for not taking a leading role in this meeting.

The astronaut from Great Britain, Dr. George Kendall, a cosmologist, kept to himself as the discussion shifted back and forth from committee proposals to budget demands to a proclamation on how important the ISS still was, especially after the disappearance of the stars and planets. He just floated there with a half-grin. The talking went on for a half hour before he cleared his throat, the last among the 40 to interject. He raised his hand along with the cough.

"Yes?" Dr. Thiel asked.

"Do you want to get their attention?" he asked to all present. There were a few affirmative grunts. "How do you get anyone's attention? Especially these governments—our governments—who have had legacies of manifest destiny, usurpation, divine right authority, colonialism, imperialism, and a lot of other *isms*?"

"Go on," Capt. Parks said.

"You take something from them that is theirs, that's how," Kendall said.

"I don't get you," volunteered Jacques Boudreaux, the Parisian.

"What's the only thing we can take from them that is theirs and ours to take?"

There were grins of realization rising en masse in the Big Tube.

"You mean us? The ISS?" asked Dr. Chun.

"But we already have it," pointed out the South African, Dr. Machlachlan.

"No," explained Dr. Kendall. "We declare ourselves a sovereign nation, independent of any nations of Earth. We close all correspondence with them until they come to us. Then we initiate diplomacy only after their act of good faith—I'm talking about getting us the hell out of here." Silence ensued.

"I like it," grinned the Texan, Capt. Parks.

"A Declaration of Independence," Dr. Thiel said softly.

"A new Bastille," added Dr. Boudreaux. "I move we name the free and independent ISS the Bastille."

"That was a prison," Parks said.

"Exactement!" the Frenchman exclaimed.

"I move we call it the Alamo," Parks said.

"There's a motion on the floor,Brian" Dr. Thiel said, but this went nowhere—only one vote was cast for "the Bastille." The Eastern hemisphere astronauts couldn't get behind the "Alamo," either. But it didn't take long for them to finally decide on the name of their independent, sovereign nation.

Babel. This time, however, it was built from the top down.

A final motion was made, discussed briefly, and then voted into law—Babel's first—by affirmation: whatever they would do they would do together, unified, and without any show of being distracted from below.

The newly promoted President of the United States conferred with his advisers, left over from the previous President who had resigned unexpectedly. He had become painfully aware of the difference in responsibilities between the Vice Presidency and the Presidency, a weight he now bore with considerable effort.

"Tell 'em to keep it," a wiry bald man advised.

"Tell 'em to just have patience," advised another who had some hair.

"Tell 'em to ask the Russians," chimed in a hard-faced woman. "They're the ones with the taxi."

The President rapped his fingers on the shiny, heavily waxed table.

"So what I'm being told, then," he said to the woman in particular, "is that it's really the Russians' responsibility?" He sighed. "The fucking Russians. Having to depend on the fucking Russians. Thanks, Barack, for shutting down the Shuttle."

"Not that again," said the wiry bald man. "He had to. It cost too much in lives."

"No," said the President, "it cost too much." No one had a comeback. "So, the Russians?"

"Certainly," she answered.

"I'm sure they'll insist on bringing their cosmonauts home first."

"How many seats does the Soyuz have?"

"Three, Mr. President," said the woman.

"How many cosmonauts are there up there?"

"Two, Mr. President," answered the man with hair.

"Well, at least they could bring another person down on the first trip."

"Or they could be fair and do a lottery to see what three go first," said the woman. "After all, we're the ones who built the whole damn thing with our Shuttles." The wiry bald man groaned.

"Well, Mr. President," he said, "they'll bring theirs home first, f'sure. I mean, what can anyone do? They're the Russians. You know how they are."

"And of course they're not going to hire out their taxi for free," added the woman. "They'll run the meter the whole time. They'll count the time in dog minutes."

"Yea," said the wiry bald man, "and guess who's gonna pay the fare for everybody else?"

"Do we have any other options?" asked the President.

"We could restock it," said the hard-faced woman, "but that would take an act of Congress."

"Yes, I know how difficult it is to get something like that to happen," the President agreed.

"No, Mr. President," she corrected him, "it would literally take an Act of Congress. All NASA business is now under the auspices of the Science and Technology Committee."

"How soon could we convene that committee?"

"On break, Mr. President," said the man with hair.

"Till when?"

"Well," added the man without hair, "the whole committee's been tabled, what with the whole universe being empty and all."

"The Russians," the woman offered again.

"The fucking Russians," said the President. "O.K., then. New business."

249 miles above the Earth, Leonid Restov decrypted the message he had just received. He and his comrade, Mikhail Anatolov, read it to themselves. The message from Roscosmos was brief but astounding:

Comrades Restov and Anatolov will — alone — take the Soyuz back to Earth immediately.

The Soyuz had three seats. Anatolov looked at Restov.

"I know," Restov said.

"I don't get it," Anatolov said. "Russians only the first trip. Just us? Is this some sort of statement of superiority? No one is even close to worthy? Or that we do it our way — or else?"

"That's thinking left over from the old regime, Mikhail. Actually, it might make sense."

"How so?"

"How would Russia explain its choice to the other nations? What geopolitical gaffe might come out of such a misstep? Alliances could be made or destroyed. A most-favored nation could be assumed and might ruin whatever international strategies were afoot."

"I guess," said Anatolov.

"Especially," added Restov, "since the other nations could fight it out for the repeat trips, leaving Russia out of the political drama."

"I don't know, Leonid," Anatolov said, still unsure. "An empty seat is a pretty tough sell for diplomacy. In fact, my friend, it's stupid."

"We could simply disobey," Restov suggested. "Just take one of the others."

"We would be disciplined severely for insubordination; or if international strategy were jeopardized by choosing one nation over another, we could be tried as traitors."

"We could send three of the others down; insist we go last. It would be hard to discipline such magnanimity."

"Or," concluded Anatolov, "we could just follow orders. The others understand orders."

"Will they?" Restov asked. "They'll know something's up as soon as we engage the pre-flight protocols, which I remind you are very noisy. It can't be done by sneaking around. And when everyone finds out a seat's going empty, it could get very ugly when everyone starts jockeying for that third seat. I can only imagine."

Restov outranked Anatolov, so he would be the one to make any decisions, although the Russian space agency had already commanded them what to do. Could the rest of the ISS be reassured that Soyuz would return, over and over, even with a sister vehicle, to finally get them all down? If that were the case, any rational, thinking passenger would surmise, then why waste a seat on such an expensive ride home now?

Later into their shifts, Restov and Anatolov met again at their console in their quarters. They each punched in codes and whispered in Russian to their loved ones from each corner of their com unit. Both men finished their calls within a minute of each other. They each placed their headsets back in their cubbies. Their faces had gone white.

"Do we know why, now, Leonid?" Anatolov asked. "I think we do."

"You heard the same thing I did, then, Mickail?"

Restov and Anatolov had worked out their code long before liftoff from Kazakhstan. Their children knew it and their spouses knew it. The information came to them in no uncertain terms. The two cosmonauts learned what the unconscionable plan was. Their disguised conversations with family revealed to them that there were no additional launches being prepared.

The Soyuz at the ISS was being commissioned for only a final one-way trip. The old regime thinking was alive and well.

Anatolov's thinking matched Restov's thought for thought. He looked into Restov's eyes. The orders were highlighted on the screen. If they ignored the message from Roscosmos — like it never existed — made it go away just like the stars, they knew that either

Russia would change plans or that they would be waiting forever for any different offers from below.

They fully expected the latter.

He followed Restov's keystrokes, and finally he watched Restov's finger linger over the delete button. Restov searched Anatolov's expressions for any objection.

"Do it, Leonid," Anatolov urged him.

Dinner that evening included heavy sedation for Anatolov and Restov, who slept soundly through the secret meeting among the others. Hours later, it was the loud disengagement of Soyuz from the ISS docking clips that finally woke them up, both of them bolting upright in immediate recognition of what was happening. They scrambled to the next ISS segment, a supply section which had a window. They saw their Soyuz falling away toward Mother Russia.

It was Babel's final gesture toward humanity — a selfless gesture toward the humanity on board, and a sarcastic one for the humanity below: Soyuz had been jettisoned empty.

Pasted to one of the three vacant seats was a simple note: *Répondez s'il vous plait: regrets only.*

The Last Seminarian

The novice who had begun his Jesuit novitiate the previous week, the day after the stars went out, had been the only one who had shown up out of the seventeen expected. After an arduous process of completing lengthy applications, being interviewed at length many times, being screened psychologically and scholastically with numerous tests, submitting endless essays, the Novice Director had called him to congratulate him on being accepted into the Society of Jesus to begin a career that would involve service to others, missionary work, an ultimate ordination, and taking vows of poverty, chastity, and obedience.

He was instructed to come with only limited clothing and personal items in a suitcase no larger than what would fit in a plane's overhead compartment. He was assigned to the 2nd floor dormitory of the seminary where the other novices, had they shown up, would have been housed. He occupied the floor alone.

He would begin his Master of Theological Studies with a 1:1 teacher-student ratio.

The night before he left, the night all the stars went away, his parents had discouraged his vocation.

"Things have changed," his father had told him. "You might just want to put things off for a year to see how all this pans out. No one knows what's next."

"What's changed?" he had asked.

"All the stars, Malcolm," his father had answered.

"What on Earth has changed?" was his rejoinder.

In spite of the uncertainties his parents feared, he had traveled with a determination that was tested by bus and rail to keep his commitment to his calling. Because of the truancy of most of the transit industry that day, it wasn't easy.

It was no reckless prediction that the Church would be decimated by a loss of faith. It was anticipated by all of the cloth that the disappearance of the cosmos beyond the moon would create this void of faith. But the feeling among the clergy was that humanity had it in them all along to cast off all deities and embrace the secular instead. An article in the Catholic magazine, *Faith*, disputed any notion that starlessness was the only culprit, opining that it was only a co-factor to jump-start the process, given our tendencies to worship celebrity and cool; that it would have happened, sooner or later.

Malcolm's first week was bizarre, he felt, because although the sudden absence of the stars was unsettling, even to those as mentally unshakeable as those who had taken vows, his schedule had begun as if nothing in the world had changed. The first mention of the occurrence wasn't even voiced out loud until the Sunday night faith sharing, a rite in the novitiate where each one in the community was encouraged to talk about his spirituality, specifically, what he had experienced bad in his daily life and what his prayers to God were like. All was considered confidential, and according to custom no comments by others were allowed. Such a prayer meeting embraced the Ignatian concept of compassionate listening.

Malcolm was frightened to death to open his mouth for his very first faith sharing. He was not confident to share anything yet, so he was determined to stay silent lest he be deemed ridiculous, even silently, compared to all of the other esteemed men of learning. He knew that, being the only novice, a stunning reality in itself, he could listen to them all first, but ultimately the community would turn to hear him before concluding. If St. Ignatius Loyola wanted compassionate listening, Malcolm vowed, then he would rise to the occasion, and when and if called upon to have his turn, at least he could rely on whatever templates of confession had been offered before his turn.

It would be a long night, for his very first faith sharing centered on the subject of the starless sky. "Bible black," Father Daniel, the first to go, described it.

Up until then, the entire seminary had been resolutely silent about the sudden heavenly upheaval, which Malcolm had fantasized as their way to avoid jinxing themselves into the only novice running away.

Fr. Daniel was the Novice Director and he spoke first to introduce the faith sharing. He started with the sign of the cross and a prayer.

"Heavenly Father," he prayed, "we are thankful for this year's novitiate class. All of him." There were some chuckles, and Malcolm would have found it funny himself had it not been about him. "We are thankful for your love and for your will, by which we will carry out our holy work. We do not question the changes in the sky, for we are anchored firmly here in our faith and our love for you. We accept your will, which will be tested by all those who look up. In the name of the Father, the Son, and the Holy Spirit," he said, crossing himself.

"Amen," answered the room of Jesuits. Father Daniel remained at the dais. He chose his next words carefully, keenly aware that what he said would have a particular impact on Malcolm.

"There were to be seventeen novices in this novitiate — it was to be our biggest class in many years. This portended well for us in the sea-change we expected in the Catholic Church in this new epoch of starless nights. But the reality is that only Malcolm has joined us." Malcolm was embarrassed, dreading the others turning to him and regarding him with welcoming smiles and approving nods. The turns, smiles, and nods, however, were not forthcoming. This gave him the uncomfortable feeling of being talked about like he wasn't even there. He squirmed in his metal folding chair, direly in need of some WD-40, and the loud creaking that betrayed his uneasiness was the thing that did prompt the turns of the others in his direction. He splinted every muscle in his buttocks into a rigid, silent poise.

"The night before his arrival the stars went away," Fr. Daniel continued. I am reminded of the writings of Diego Lainez, an early Jesuit, who wrote about how Ignatius would go to the roof of the Jesuit headquarters in Rome and would be still — absolutely silent. He'd take off his hat and gaze heavenly at the sky. Suddenly, he'd fall to his knees, praising God in silent tears.

"To Ignatius, the stars were a gift from God. I now pray that I shall find God in all of the other things from which the stars have distracted me. The spiritual exercise trains us to see God in all things. Perhaps now we can be even less burdened in our attempts to do so. No matter what else anyone has to say, we should consider the astronomical phenomenon as a blessing in some way. We've held our tongues long enough, my brothers, and it is of spiritual relevance, I think, so I invite all to embrace the blessing reverently, acceptingly, and — at this time — vocally."

Priest after Brother all showed similar devotions to the Ignatius Spiritualism in their faith sharing. Everyone also related the disappearance of the stars to his devotion in some clever way. Malcolm began to get caught up in it, but occasionally his mind whirred. He felt it was stupid that he was more worried about what he'd say about the stars leaving than about the actual leaving of the stars.

There were two persons left to share. One was the Spiritual Director, Fr. Lucas, the other himself. After an uncomfortable and awkward silence, Malcolm felt Fr. Lucas was going to punt, so he began to speak. To his surprise, Fr. Lucas silenced him with a finger to his lips.

"Malcolm and I," he then said, "will share at our next meeting."

Malcolm was relieved, but also felt a bit robbed out of his first moment to impress his teachers.

The community prayed the Our Father and then adjourned for the evening, some of the older priests to play cards, others to pray privately before retiring. Martin and Fr. Lucas ascended the stairs to the second floor where Malcolm's room was.

They entered his bedroom, which sported a small closet, a single bed, a cleared desk and a small crucifix on the wall. Malcolm sat on his bed and extended an arm indicating Fr. Lucas to sit on the desk chair.

"Well, your first Faith Sharing, Malcolm. What did you think?"

"I think," Malcolm said quietly, "it was beautiful. So many learned men and so uniform a reaction. And the way they all tied in the stars was so inspiring. If there were a transcript of everything said, I would treasure it. I think this Jesuit community is rock solid and uniform in its dedication to Ignatius. I'm so thrilled to be a part of it."

"And I think," Fr. Lucas said, stroking the hair of his trim, neat goatee, "that it was horseshit." Malcolm's mouth dropped open. "You heard me," Fr. Lucas pressed.

"I know what you said, Father," Malcolm agreed. "I just don't believe my own ears."

"We're Jesuits, Malcolm," Fr. Lucas said sternly. A vein on his forehead swelled. Malcolm knew the look he saw on his face. It was the look of someone about to unload after bottling everything up too long. "We're the intelligentsia of the Catholic Church," Fr. Lucas continued. "We're the ones who reconverted half of Europe after that lunatic Luther stole it away from us. There are 35 craters on the moon named for Jesuit scientists. We backed DaVinci. We discovered quinine. We've educated Descartes, Voltaire, and James Joyce. This is not a phenomenon that can be explained by even those smart enough to have craters named after them. It cannot offer itself as just some Ignatian exercise. This is God himself at work. We're being told something. We're being told that no matter how smart we think we are, we should sometimes realize that we haven't been selected as the chosen ones to know it all. We're being messed with, Malcolm, and I don't know how I feel about that just yet. Just when we think we're doing God's work...or will...or whatever you want to call our mission, he steps in and says to us, 'God is bigger than your Ignatian Spirituality,' and, 'God is bigger than your Society, even Catholicism.' I don't care if I ever hear another cricket or a babbling brook or another bird singing. I want to know what God did with our stars! And I want to know why! God's will? We're O.K. with that? I'm not O.K. with it. Are you O.K. with it? When are we ever going to be let in on the plan?"

"Excuse me, Father, but *our* stars? Do you think God actually did something to them?"

"They're not here now, are they? They were here before you came and now that you're here, they're all gone. Aren't they, Malcolm?" Fr. Lucas tilted his head and looked at him askew.

Malcolm began an uncomfortable sensation not unlike anger. Just what was Fr. Lucas saying? That he had anything to do with this?

"God created the universe," Malcolm began.

"And God can surely tinker with it at will, can't he?" Fr. Lucas interrupted sarcastically.

"No," answered Malcolm, "he actually cannot just tinker with it." Malcolm's tone was stern, even reprimanding, but he didn't care, for he didn't care at all for Fr. Lucas' tone, which skitted dangerously close to saying Malcolm somehow was part of the cataclysm.

Fr. Lucas' pupils constricted, easy to notice because of his light blue eyes. His face went rigid, elongating, dramatizing his deep, vertical wrinkles and the menacing shadows they created, like a Halloween flashlight shining from the chin up. His eyebrows furrowed. He began kneading his hands briskly together, as if they were suddenly cold and he needed to generate heat. His armpits wore moist circles.

Malcolm watched, uncertain what to say or do.

"Fr. Lucas," he offered, "let's think about St. Ignatius. Be comforted by him."

"I'm sick to death of St. Ignatius," he said abruptly and harshly.

"Then I think you're in the wrong Order. Do you like puppies, Father? Perhaps you should try the Franciscans?"

It was a lashing out over what Fr. Lucas had insinuated about him and had said about St. Ignatius, the man who was the basis of Malcolm's entire spiritual life. It was a spinal reaction, his frontal lobes having nothing to do with it. It was a spiritual reaction. He realized as soon as he said it that it was regrettable.

Fr. Lucas quickly raised a fisted hand to strike Malcolm, but Fr. Lucas was elderly and Malcolm was young and strong. It didn't take much to grasp the striking arm in mid-swing. Fr. Lucas squirmed his arm rebelliously and glared at Malcolm.

Malcolm swallowed and then summoned all of his patience and compassion for a great man who had obviously snapped. He also tried very hard to summon his love for Fr. Lucas. He felt he had done enough Ignatian compassionate listening, and now it was time to engage the old priest in the most pure exhibition of what elusive Ignatian compassionate love he could muster.

"Forgive me, Fr. Lucas," Malcolm asked, and he slowly forced the priest's arm down until it loosened, watching his face intently until the old man was no longer showing his teeth. He released his hold to demonstrate trust, and then he immediately replaced it with a gentle grasp of reassurance. The vein in Fr. Lucas' forehead drained flat, and this was a good sign. His brow unfurrowed and the beauty of infinite calm swept his face.

"God created the universe," Malcolm began, "lovingly and intelligently, and he did it for all who can come to know him. But the real brilliance of the creation was that it was not magic. It was physics, and God let it unfold, and it did, beautifully, by following all of the rules. This is why sometimes bad things happen. Otherwise, it really would be magic and magic's no good for a loving relationship with God. If God created all of us to share in his love, would it do if most of us only loved him because of the magical things he would do every time someone prayed for a new Mercedes?"

Fr. Lucas sat stunned. Checkmated, he seemed to reconstitute himself. Silent tears like those of St. Ignatius on the Jesuit headquarters roof in Rome streaked down his cheeks. Malcolm also saw this as a good sign.

"For whatever reason the stars went out," Malcolm concluded, "it's not because God magically plucked them all away; it's because of physics. I don't know how. No one can. Perhaps we should leave that investigation to Jesuits smart enough to have craters named after them, and like Fr. Daniel said, take it as the blessing it is."

Fr. Lucas dried his eyes with his long, black cassock sleeves and turned squarely to Malcolm.

"Thank you, Novice Malcolm," he said to him. "I will be taking a leave of absence tomorrow. You see, the laws of physics have conspired to attack my faith and what used to be my comfort zone. So there'll be one less Jesuit here, more than made up by our new novice. You." Malcolm was saddened.

"Father, please—"

"No, don't, my son," Fr. Lucas kindly stopped him, now placing his hand on Malcolm's shoulder. "I apologize for my behavior. This has certainly brought out a lot of weird reactions around the whole world, and I guess I'm no exception. I'll be back. One day. In the meantime, our order is in good hands. I know it is, because you and the rest will all follow the rules. The rules of physics and the rules of the Church. We Catholics are famous for rules. The Ten Commandments, the Six Laws of the Church, the Golden Rule, even the Beatitudes. They are our scaffold. They are actually our entire religion when one thinks about it."

"No, Father," Malcolm said. "I stand behind my position that rules are good for physics and math and playgrounds, but I also stand behind the proposition that through them God shows his own love for us. For there to be religion, though, there's something else. For there to be religion, it has to be the love we show for him."

"I'm happy for you, Malcolm. I really am. If and when I can be as accepting as you, I'll come back. In the meantime, think about what I said. We've been challenged with something that doesn't seem to follow the rules."

"No, Father, we really have been blessed with it. When you accept that, you'll be back."

"I hope soon, Malcolm. I surely hope soon."

"I'll pray for you, Father," Malcolm called to Fr. Lucas as he started to walk out of the room. He stopped and turned around to face Malcolm.

"No, Malcolm, pray for everyone."

"I will, Father. But that still includes praying for you."

The old priest turned again to walk out of the room. Malcolm could hear his steps beyond the door, which didn't take the flight of stairs up; instead, he could hear them descend to the first floor. A moment later he heard the front door open and close.

Stars, faith, and now Fr. Lucas, Malcolm thought to himself. *Here one minute…*

The Contestant

[Applause.] "Guns and beautiful women in bikinis, Mel. It doesn't get any better than this. It's always sold well."

"Right, Big Bob. Welcome, everyone, I'm Mel Manrod."

"And I'm Big Bob Wynotski." [Applause.]

"When the Miss America pageant announced that it would no longer feature the bathing suit phase in the competition, Big Bob, the NRA knew its time had come. Ever since Charlton Heston's "cold, dead hands" were pried from his rifle, we wanted to get nearly naked women into the mix." [Applause.]

"Or women nearly naked, Mel." [Laughter.]

"Or naked women near, Big Bob—" [Laughter] "—and I suppose we could milk that joke some more, but ladies and gentlemen, for the first time, welcome, all of you, to the Miss NRA Beauty Pageant." [Applause.] "Guns are for everyone, men, women, and properly instructed children. Why should beautiful women be left out? You see them in TV crime dramas. In bikinis with their smoking pistols. You see them on crime magazine covers. In their bras. Where are they in real life? Ladies and gentlemen, they are here—here, tonight! [Applause.] "Please extend a warm, smoking welcome as they pass in review on our "gunway." [Applause.]

"Yes, Mel, these are uncertain times, aren't they?"

"Yes, Big Bob, they sure are. Unrest in the streets, illegals everywhere, and now this star malarkey. Waddaya think?"

"Who the hell knows—am I right? Holy moly! I mean, they're here. Then they're gone."

"Like our guns, Big Bob."

"Ain't that the truth, Mel. That's what some smellocrats would like to do. Gone. All gone."

"Not on our watch, Big Bob." [Applause.]

"No siree, Mel."

"Say, Big Bob, here's a segue for ya."

"Yea?"

"Yea. At the Q n' A portion here, we ask the girls the following question: What the hell happened to the stars? And could our guns be next?"

"It'll be interesting to hear these gals weigh in, Mel. They're pissed."

"You bet. And heavily armed. And oh, by the way, in case anyone missed it, tonight's winner—the first ever crowned Miss NRA, will receive an incredible prize."

"You said it, Mel, tell 'em what she'll win."

"Yea, Big Bob. It's Adolph Hitler's Golden Walther PP, valued at over $200,000." [Audience gushes.]

"Boy, Mel, I'd put on a bikini myself to win that." [Laughter.]

"Please don't. I'd give it to you to *not* put on a bikini." [Laughter morphs into applause.]

"Ha!"

"Ha ha!"

"All kidding aside, Mel, let's get ready for the first contestant, Miss Smith and Wesson. Thanks, everyone, but please quiet down. Miss Smith and Wesson, what the hell happened to the stars? Could our guns be next?"

Miss Smith & Wesson: "Yes, I think it's important to know what happened to the stars. The more we learn about anything, the better America gets. Knowing about stars can really help our country. We have the smartest scientists — am I right? — and they're on it, America." [Applause.] "The importance of the stars and what happened is very important, and we will find out, because it is very important. I for one think that knowing about the stars can really help our country. Am I right? Thank you. And God bless America, and God bless the NRA. Am I right?" [Applause.]

"Miss AK-47?"

Miss AK-47: "Well, I think we all want to know what happened to the stars. They probably just all burned out. I mean, they can't last forever. Nothing lasts forever, except the 2nd Amendment." [Applause.] "But I have to say that just because the stars burned out, that doesn't mean that we should give up. We should keep trying. We can make our own stars. We have the 2nd Amendment, so we can do anything we want. We can even make a second 2nd Amendment if we want!" [She ululates and raises her AK-47 into the air.] "Or else!" [Applause. Miss AK-47 fires into the air. Some ceiling tiles fall onto the stage. Applause suddenly dips, then resumes stronger.]

"Man, I'd like to—"

"Watch it, Mel."

"Whew, yea, thanks, Big Bob."

"Miss M-16?"

Miss M-16: "No one knows, but should we care? I mean, look at the girls here tonight." [Applause.] "They're not worried about the stupid stars. They're focused. It takes a lot of focus and discipline to go the distance all the way up to the Miss NRA pageant. If you ask me, all these girls are the stars. And their guns are the rings around the stars." [Applause. All the girls brandish their arms and abruptly lock and load.]

"They're cocky tonight, Big Bob." [Laughter.]

"They sure are, Mel, and ready to stand their ground, so — ladies, hold on there, Missies, we're in Atlantic City, not Tallahassee!" [Laughter until a round fires off, ricochets.]

"Whoa! Remember, girls, we're just the messengers." [Laughter.] "Big Bob, bring out Miss Sniper, will ya?"

"Miss Sniper, what's the story here? No stars, so, our guns next?"

Miss Sniper: "Oh, well, I think they're still there. I think that gravity is very mysterious and we don't know all about things like gravity and dark stuff and nematodes or other things from the Amazon. We'll find out really soon what it is about the stars. I know it. This is America, and I know we will do it before anyone else, and then look out, world." [Applause.] "We will because we're the home of the brave and the land of the free." [Applause.]

"How 'bout you, Miss Beretta? What the hell happened to the stars? Could our guns be next?"

Miss Beretta: "Albert Einstein said genius is 20% perspiration and 85% imagination. We should all just use our perspiration more and we'll come up with the reason. If it worked for Einstein, it'll work for America. I know, because Einstein wasn't just a genius —

he was an American!" [Applause] "And he had a whole lot of guns. Look it up—it's a fact. God bless America." [Applause.]

"Miss Luger?"

Miss Luger: "I probably shouldn't be saying this on TV—I don't even know if such a thing is classified or top secret or anything like that, but my brother has a friend who works for the weather channel and he says there's a lot of really weird things going on with the radar. Like there are things parked in front of the stars, blocking them out. Well, girls—and judges—there really can't be too many things that'll do something like that, and if this is a UFO invasion, I pledge that if I win I will be honored to represent America as a goodwill ambassador to the aliens." [Applause.] "And if that doesn't work, I will do my share as a soldier for our cause, because I'll be packin'," [Applause] "and because our cause is right, and because might makes it right." [Applause.]

"Miss Derringer? Why'd the stars disappear? Are our guns next?"

Miss Derringer: "They have? They did? When did that happen? Thank you." [Anemic applause.]

"Miss Howitzer?"

Miss Howitzer: "I think this is definitely a sign from God. He wants us to look up, because he's going to be showing us something really special soon. I know it's going to be Jesus coming down in all his glory. And looking at what's going on in the Middle East and Russia and the Democrats and all, it's about time. Won't all those people without guns be sorry!" [Applause.]

"Miss Saturday Night Special?"

Miss Saturday Night Special: "I'm sorry, but I'm not really qualified to talk about the stars. But what I am qualified to do is tell you how great this gun-totin' country is." [Applause.] "Why, did you know that each and every day, a thousand honor students volunteer at old people's homes to wash their cars and mow their lawns and clean their guns? And they don't even want to be paid.

My agent says that's just stupid — working for nothin' — but I disagree. Everyone should work for free. Imagine what a wonderful world this would be!" [Applause.] "And if the stars — oh, what? Oh, I'm out of time? Can I just say — what? I can't. Oh, I'm sorry. Oh, O.K." [Applause.]

"Miss Self-Defense?"

Miss Self-Defense: "I think that something just happened to their flickering. No one talks about that. They're just flickering much, much too slow now. On, off, on, off, on, off, on, off, on, off…and when you slow it down, you're going to have a longer time with them off. Any time now they're going to flick bright again, and it'll keep on doing this really slow until it speeds back up again. If you want flashes in the dark, there's nothing like strafing that home invader in the dark. I've done it myself twelve times already." [Applause.] "That's what the 2nd Amendment is for." [Applause.] "Go 2nd Amendment!" [Applause.] "God bless America." [Applause.]

"Inspiring, Miss Self-Defense, inspiring. What about you, Miss Shoot-from-the-Hip?"

Miss Shoot-from-the-Hip: "Well, Mel, that's a doozy of a question. Really! This is a beauty pageant for God's sake. Our expertise is makeup, hairspray, and revealing bathing suits that really aren't all that revealing if you're looking for nipples — and I know you are!" [Applause.]

"I know I am."

"Me, too, Big Bob." [Laughter.]

Miss Shoot-from-the-Hip: "And everyone gets up here and says, 'God bless America,' and, 'Yay, us!' And then you want us to give opinions on a phenomenon that even NASA is still clueless about? You want us to discuss our feelings about an astronomical event of cosmic proportions? I don't know about the rest of you gals, but I didn't get my Ph.D. in stellar astronomy. If anyone else has, please be my guest and step up. Not you, Miss *Jesus-is-coming*.

And not you, *Miss Perspiring Einstein*. We're not here to give all the scientists a Eureka! moment. That's not our job. We're here to look good, sound good, walk good, and just be hot women with guns. What do I think about the stars! As if! Yea, America, you heard it here first—it's God, it's Jesus, they burned out, it's a frickin' UFO invasion! Are you all nuts? Have you all lost your fucking minds? Thank you and God bless America." [Audience collectively gasps, then slow clap begins, falters, stops.]

"I just want to say what a disgrace all that was, Mel." [Polite applause.]

"I don't know, Big Bob. I'm thinking, wow, all that—and brains, too!"

"I don't think you want 'em for their brains, Mel." [Laughter.] "C'mon, Miss Shoot-from-the-Hip, you're better than that. We're better than that. America is better than that." [Applause.] "I think Miss Shoot-from-the-Hip needs a group hug, huh, girls? Waddaya say?" [Applause.] "Come on, Miss Shoot-from-the-Hip, don't be shy now. Oh, are you armed, too, Miss Shoot-from-the-Hip?"

"I think they all are, Big Bob. Me, too."

"You know I am."

"Makes you wonder if we'll ever have some kinda mass shooting at this pageant."

"Guns don't kill people, Mel, women do." [Applause.]

"If it's gonna happen, better by hot chicks with their big guns. That's just hot!" [Applause continues.]

"What about the stars, Mel?"

"Big Bob, 'less you're talkin' 'bout shootin' stars, I've forgotten all about 'em. Thanks, though to everyone for not forgetting 'bout us and for watching. We'll have the decision of our judges right after these important messages from the NRA. Oh, wait—what's this? Ladies and gentlemen, I've just been informed that one of our judges is no longer with us tonight, and we'll have more information as...." [Applause and programming fades out.]

The Schizophrenic

Kate knew she was crazy. She had been crazy since her first year of high school when the strangers began visiting her and told her what to do. Diagnosed with schizophrenia, she had done well on her medications and currently was functional in her clerical employment. The visitors came less frequently but their disembodied voices still called to her. When she had the right prescription she could defy them and refuse their bidding. There had been no office episodes at work nor any public psychotic breaks, but she well knew of what she was capable. Her pills were so important: take some in the morning, some at night, some on a full stomach, some on an empty stomach; and the regimen worked so much better when she had a good night's sleep.

She lived alone in a one bedroom apartment that sat over an elderly man's unattached garage. She liked that. She could pace. She could clomp around as much as she needed and there would be no one below to complain. She could play music as loud as she pleased, except that she hated loud music and found it unpleasing. But if she wanted, she could, and that was what mattered. A garage filled with the memorabilia of another person's life buffered her from the rest of the world. One would have to slog through his entire life's story to reach her. Hopefully, her visitors would be exhausted by the time they got to her.

What this really meant — what was important to her — was that she could scream and no one would hear it. One might think if a scream were necessary, it would be a bad thing if no one could hear it. In her case, however, it was a good thing because it happened so often. Whenever the screaming increased in frequency, she knew it was time for a change of prescription.

When she saw the ghost she did not scream. She was not troubled. It had been a long time since a stranger had come to visit, so she figured it might just be time for a new medication. She hoped the people who made medicine would keep inventing the new ones as quickly as the old ones stopped working. She ignored her ghost which was particularly gruesome. It appeared gouged about its head and was bloody everywhere. There was drool.

It tried to get her attention. She would turn and it would slip back in front of her. She would turn again and it would repeat the maneuver. She looked into the mirror and it was in the reflection behind her in a threatening pose. She had seen all of these tricks before. She continued to ignore it.

She wanted to get ready for bed. She had had a very busy day and was tired. She didn't appreciate that someone or something was trying to keep her from her night's sleep, which was so important in balancing her medications. She walked to the window of her bedroom and pulled the curtains back. The apparition suddenly appeared outside her window as if it had climbed a magic ladder. How many times, she wondered, had it spied on her? It was all she could do to stare defiantly right through it. The stars twinkled brightly and clearly in the sky on this last night they ever would.

"Beautiful night," she said out loud to no one, rudely ignoring her visitor. "Not a cloud in the sky. And my, what stars!" This had broken the seal, for her voices never initiated conversation, only responding with counter-arguments urging her on to bad choices.

"You know I'm here, Kate." She tossed the curtains together abruptly. "Did you hear me, Kate?" She turned around sharply and there it stood again in front of her. "I said that you know I'm here. How rude, Kate. Don't ignore me. That won't work this time." She finally fixed her eyes on it and took in the full impact of its appearance. This one was a very troubling sight, indeed. It appeared pleased to get her attention.

She refused to scream. It still would take way more than this, she vowed, to make her scream. Not even the smell of the rot that accompanied her visitor. Or even the aftersmell of vomited rice. No solitary ghost ever could compete with some of the bizarre things her diseased brain had conjured up for her in the past. Things that fed at the deepest troughs of her mind. Terrible things. Horrifying images and morbid tableaus. Things that brought out her most excellent screams. She had made great strides, however, even to the point where she could not only suppress her screams, but actually argue away her hallucinations.

"I know you're not real," she told the ghost finally. It was fuzzy, semi-transparent, and wore a face of mischief through its disfiguring facial gore.

"Just how do you know I'm not real, Kate?" it asked her. Its voice was deep and tremulous. The reverb, she felt, was a bit of a cliché and over the top.

"How do I know? Well, first of all, seeing ghosts is just plain crazy. But crazy is not reality. If ghosts were reality, I'd be carpooling with some every day to work. And there are a lot of crazy people to keep ghosts popping up in what folks hear. Ghosts in their houses and weird noises from their attics. Even people not as crazy as me say they see ghosts. There's even a TV show about it."

"Ah," said the ghost, "a reality show. What was that you were saying now?"

"Seeing ghosts is not reality. Ghosts ain't real, ghost. Shadows, sneaky reflections, sounds from the attic, creepy feelings. I'm not buying it. I'm not falling for any of it. It's just the buried crazy part of someone that comes out when they see one. And another good reason I know you're not real is because I'm already crazy to start with. So seeing 'em is crazy and I'm crazy. Crazier than most people who say they've seen ghosts. So what do you think? Are you real? My crazy ain't buried so deep you see, so I'm liable to see anything. Don't feel so special."

"But you are up to date on your meds, aren't you? Have you missed a dose, perhaps?"

"No. I'm good at taking my medicine. But then there's you..." Kate said timidly, her voice fading to a frightened whisper.

"Then if you've been taking all your medicine, then you're well. It's not because you're crazy, is it, that I'm here? You're being treated. I must be the real deal."

"Seeing ghosts is still crazy, crazy ghost. Even with my meds going good. There ain't no such things as ghosts, anyway. Haven't you heard?"

"Oh, I've heard. But now I'm not buying it." The ghost patted itself briskly up and down, tufts of dust and wafts of malodor erupting with each slap. "I'm here. Plain as day. Just like you, Kate. A phantom — a wraith, true, but real as you and troubled by unfinished business."

"Then you're dead if you're a ghost."

"Ouch."

"Well, you said it, not me. What's your unfinished business, ghost?"

"Tell me, Kate, have you seen the stars lately?"

"Yes. You know I did. You were right out there in the window when I did."

"No, Kate, they're gone."

"Oh, they're there," she insisted.

"No, Kate, they're gone. Take another look."

She walked back over to the same window, and when she parted the curtains again the sky was ink black. Again the ghost appeared outside her window, looking in at her. He raised a mangled hand to point up. She followed his aim to a starless sky.

"It's overcast," she said, "and they're above the clouds."

"No, Kate. They're not above the clouds. There are no clouds. Not tonight. You said so yourself. Not a cloud in the sky, you said. My, what stars, you said." She strained to look but saw no stars at all. Were they really gone or was this just part of the hallucination that had ferried her ghost to her?

"No stars is crazy, too," she said. "I see you and I don't see them—the same thing if you ask me. One thing's as crazy as the other."

"No, Kate, they are no longer shining in the sky for you. But they're around, trust me. They're just hiding."

"Hiding where?"

"Kate, you know where. They're in the place no one dares to look."

"Riddles and games. I don't know what you're talking about, ghost."

"Those deepest places where your deepest thoughts are. Your scary thoughts, Kate. Ugly thoughts. Dangerous thoughts. Things you want to do but know you must not."

Kate waited. She did not like what the ghost was saying. These things were hurtful things, for she had seen her deepest thoughts. She had heard her deepest voices. Thoughts and voices about scary things, ugly things, and dangerous things. Things she used the rest of her mind to suppress.

"You need to leave, ghost," she said.

"But if I go, who will remind you of your deepest thoughts? They are you, aren't they? Don't you want to be yourself? Most people go through life trying to find themselves, but you live to deny your true self. Don't you need to be you? Self-actualization, Kate. What would Maslow say?"

"I don't know any Maslow, and I don't want to be the real me. No. I want to be someone else."

"Who, Kate? Who else do you want to be?"

"The person I should have been all along, before my sickness."

"That's not you, Kate. You need to be your real person. How dare they tell you not to be you? You can show them, Kate. Show 'em good."

"Stop, crazy ghost. Leave me. Go away."

"Do you want me to go where the stars went? Do you want to go where the stars are?"

The thought of that gave Kate a strange sense of comfort. "Yes," she muttered to herself, "that would be nice. That would be normal. Like everything used to be." She was thankful that the stars had always been there for all of us. For her. It didn't matter where they were. They promised the same world the next day, day after day, in a universe that remained constant and familiar. A stable universe. Something she could wake up to each morning. Home. Reality. The ghost spotted the hearth burning warmly in her eyes.

"Ah, then, yes, Kate. Very good. Join me there. You see, the stars are our innermost thoughts. The thoughts that you think it is good to suppress, but it's not good to do that. They are what are normal, what we all are. And when we bury our real selves so deep we're not ourselves anymore. The stars are like the canary in the mine. Do you see, Kate?"

"Yes," Kate replied. "I do." She paused. She reflected. A troubled look of conflict passed over her face. *This is how they always trick me*, she thought.

"Don't think, Kate. Do. Act on your impulses."

"No, crazy ghost. I'm better than that."

"Better than your real self?"

"We were born with Original Sin, ghost. We're better than that now. Our real selves were the sinners. The original sinners. We can do better. I can do better. I know better."

"That's religion talking, Kate. That went away with the stars. The canary suffocated on it."

"No, ghost, we've been warned not to go back to being our real selves. Our deepest selves."

"Oh, Kate, you're being foolish. When you deny your real self, you're denying what God has made you."

"God? Like God has anything to do with you! You bring up God? Now...how dare *you*?"

"God's with the stars, Kate. Our deepest ugliest, scariest thoughts created him. Created religion. Santa Claus, magic, and luck. It's all make-believe."

"And you, ghost, are you real? Or make-believe?"

The ghost paused now. "That is a trick question, Kate."

"Is it now? God's not real but you are? You come from my deepest thoughts and fears, too, ghost. You can't have it both ways. Now I'm going to tell you this just one more time."

"Yes?"

"Leave. Go back into my deepest thoughts and fears and worries. Stay there. And then I'll throw away the key." The ghost pouted.

"Eve was a great woman, Kate. Even she took the apple — why can't you?"

"Goodbye," Kate told the ghost.

"I'll go. But I'll be back. You'll see."

"Perhaps," Kate replied. "I take every day one day at a time." She smiled, and added, "Just like my medicine."

"You and your goddamned medicine! Fool! You killed your own canary! You!"

"Goodbye. And really, don't come back."

"You wish!" said the fuzzy, transparent shade, becoming more transparent and fuzzier the angrier he became, its mischievous face replaced by one of vindictiveness. "I will come back," it promised. "You know I will," it seethed.

"You usually do," she replied, and then the specter faded away altogether.

Kate turned to draw her bath and looked forward to the renewal the water would bring. After that, she planned on retiring for the night. The next morning she would take her daily medicine, and the next evening she would know that everything was alright if she saw the stars in the sky again. She felt good. A day without screaming.

It had been another good day.

The Life and Times of Climax Johnson

Climax Johnson had never regretted being named Climax Johnson — Johnson after who his father was — and Climax after what his father did. In his brief two dozen trips around the Sun in, of all things, the Sunshine State, he had lived several lifetimes.

He had been a POW during the War on Drugs, serving four years at a Federal Camp in Florida for trafficking cocaine. Although the amount confiscated had been less than the 28 grams that would have made him eligible for just a diversion program, the integrity of his contraband was judged to be pure enough that nothing else but cutting it and redistributing it in diluted amounts could be the intended purpose. A *gotcha!* moment for the prosecutor.

Off he went.

For the better part of forty-one months he made twelve cents per hour by day, weed-whacking the U.S. Navy base in Pensacola. For the better part of four years, back at the dorm, he never saw the stars at night because the light pollution, designed to keep the camera eyes within f-stop tolerances, washed them out totally in search of any inmate indiscretions. Like always, he never really thought about the stars.

Out of sight, out of mind.

One day he was watching the only national news someone had decreed would be the one to watch — and this hadn't changed in years — when two particular reports pricked his interest. The first was a report that there had been an explosion at the Santa Rosa county jail in Millville. This was the place where inmates were sent if they committed any infractions. It caught his attention because he had people from his cubicle there. The TV was of the cathode ray variety, hanging heavily and dangerously in the rec room in one corner, with five rows of pews placed in front of it. The story was local, but because it involved inmates, it made the national news. On *Robin Meade and Friends*, the CNN breakfast and *breaking* news/entertainment hybrid, Robin Meade reported it straight into the ears of Climax Johnson. She offered her vanilla report with beauty-pageant sparkle, reporting that two inmates had been killed in the explosion, but then emphasized her relief that, "Thank God none of them escaped."

"Looks like two of 'em did," Climax said out loud.

The other report was that there would be something called a conjunction that night, that Jupiter, Mars, and Venus would share a small patch of sky at the same time.

"I think I'd like to see this conjunction thing," he said to his buddy to his right. "I don't think I've ever seen three planets at once. Hell, not even another planet. I'd like to see that."

"Four planets," his buddy said.

"No, three," Climax reaffirmed, sure of what he had heard.

"Four," again from his buddy.

"I don't feel ya," Climax said.

"If ya catch the Earth's horizon out the corner of ya eye at the same time that ya see the other three, then ya seeing four—ya understandin' what I'm sayin'? Ya follow?"

"Oh," Climax said. "Yea. That's something. Yea, I'd like to see that."

Climax didn't get to see his three- or four-planet conjunction. The same problem, the camp's light pollution, kept any stars or planets invisible the entire time he was there, notwithstanding conjunctions. On the night before his release, he once again looked up and saw the false lights of the camp. No stars. *Not here, f'sure*, he thought.

He wouldn't have anyway, because the night before he was released was the night the stars vanished.

"Tomorrow night. I'll see y'all tomorrow night," he promised, waving his finger into the sky. News—even cosmic news—traveled slowly in the justice system.

Climax had nearly a four-year head start on the rest of mankind when he looked up on his first night of freedom and still saw nothing. This time, instead of seeing the skyglow and whiteout of the camp's wide-spectrum LED lamps, he saw the black sky, just as empty.

On his first night of freedom, he sat on a knoll and continued to look up. He wanted his eyes to adjust to the dark. He had heard the media filled with the reports of celestial disruptions and stellar abdication, but the stars had never been a part of his world anyway. Nevertheless, he kept looking deeper and deeper into the skies for anything. He knew they were there before he had gone to prison, not that he cared. In fact, he couldn't ever remember watching for the stars before. He always had to keep his eyes level with the terrain in his neighborhood, always focused on a sweep of 60° but with peripheral vision alert to movement. That was just survival. When he was older and began his sexual athletics, he was only in it for the skin rides, which squandered any romance like gazing dreamily at starry skies. Older than that put him into urban glare. But here where he should normally see the swath of the Milky Way and everything with it, he saw only black.

He soul-searched. He bobbed for epiphanies. He attempted self-analysis. He waxed contemplative. Without knowing it, he plugged himself into the Maslow pyramid toward self-actualization, but his pyramid had only the first two tiers. He introspected. He reminisced.

The blackness segued to nostalgia, transporting his mind to his childhood. Before they had been shot, his two older brothers would take him to the matinee on Saturdays to see blaxploitation movies. His sister went with them, but usually hung out by the ticket kiosk to cherry pick desperately oversexed boys from the cafeteria line passing in revue. His little brother was still in his momma's belly, the belly of his only known parent. He would never meet his little brother. Everybody important to him was gone.

Everybody, including the stars. *God'a'mighty punishing me*, he thought.

He had been released months early with his accrued good time. He returned to his old neighborhood in Miami and to all of its temptations, which quickly relieved him of his $700 of weed-whacking earnings, a good portion of it, ironically, spent on weed. When he found he needed more money, the mockery of his freedom was that after he had paid his debt to society his felony had branded him a pariah. This reduced his employment prospects to things that had created his debt to society in the first place. The likelihood was that if he stayed in Miami, his freedom would be nothing more than an entr'acte between the previous and the next incarceration. There, his likely recidivism meant there was little sense in investing any time in seeking gainful employment.

He needed to move on. There was no moss to gather in Miami. Also, he didn't want to fight the Feds again on any level. They fight dirty. He knew he was dirty, too, but their kind of dirty fighting was the kind you couldn't fight. He cut his ties with his fellow drug dealers and became a conscientious objector in the War on Drugs.

He landed in Tampa, hung out at clubs, assisted the DJs at their mixing consoles, mingled with the roadies, and had sex with women who thought he was with the crew. He thought that DJ'ing could make him an honest living, get him laid, and—bonus—didn't even require a background check. And he could spin music. How leet was that? But Climax had no equipment and such gear was never loaned out to the likes of him.

He searched any and all jobs that had anything to do with music, but since he actually played no instruments, he had to filter the search down to playing the music of people who actually did play. Then he saw the ad on the city bus advert:.

> *Wanted: groovy and fab guy to play sweet sounds for WEMD.*
> *Inquire at studio.*

He had discovered that the blaxploitation movies were right about white people, so he generally steered clear of them. *Groovy* and *fab*—these were white words.

I'm groovy and fab, he thought. *F'sure groovy and fab enough for this white job.* He wrote down the address, got off of the bus, and walked until he reached the building that housed the radio station. The address was a three-story slot of brownstone between two other brownstones. He entered the main entrance into the foyer and read the placard:

> Vlad's Tattoo and Piercing, first floor; Madame Kismét, Seer and Psychic Surgeon, second floor; WEMD Radio, third floor.

The place smelled like what was inside a vacuum cleaner bag. He took short, shallow breaths and began to wind his way up squeaky stairs that had a rickety bannister. He didn't even notice Vlad's on the first floor, but on the second he stopped to consider Madame Kismét.

She was a woman.

Her door was open. He peaked in and there was Madame Kismét herself, bundled on a sofa, knees up high, painting her toenails. She had her foot perched on the edge of a coffee table that had a sugar bowl, a pot, a coffee cup, and a steak knife. She had little cotton balls stuffed between each toe. She was overweight and Climax noticed this was posing some difficulty for her. She looked up.

"Can I help you?" she asked.

"I was wondering if I could help you," he said. "I could finish the last few toes." She looked him up and down. "I like women's feet," he added.

"Really?" she asked suspiciously.

"A lot," he answered. She hesitated a moment, then smiled.

"Come on in," she offered. She was white and fat, he noted, but fat, white women were the best, so he entered. He sniffed cautiously. The vacuum bag smell was overwhelmed by the waft and ebb of patchouli. She held out the small bottle of nail polish and brush and he took them.

"Bible Black, huh?" he said. Then he looked at her toes again. He regarded her three unpainted ones. "They were red before. Why black now?"

"In honor of our new sky. You have no idea how business has taken off since the stars burned out."

"Really?" he asked, looking around her empty establishment.

"Yea, really," she snapped. "And I like my nails like I like my men," she added matter-of-factly.

"You liked red men before?" he asked.

She put her feet down and reached over the coffee table to pour some hot coffee into the cup. She plopped in two sugar cubes and then reached for the steak knife to stir it. "I like my coffee black, too." She paused to look back up at Climax and smiled a peculiar smile. "I like my coffee like I like my men," she said, continuing to stir the cup with the knife. "Black with a knife in 'em." Climax let it go. "Want some coffee yourself?" she offered. He saw grounds floating on top of the coffee in her cup.

"Nah, it's all good."

"Hope you didn't mind me having some."

"It's your place," he said as she put her unfinished set of toes back up on the coffee table edge and waved them at Climax. The little cotton balls were hanging in there.

"Now go to it. Paint."

Climax hunched down over the small table from the other side and began on her middle toe on her right foot, continuing in her initial direction. He moved on to the fourth toe and finally her pinkie. He pushed the brush all the way into the bottle and screwed its cap on tightly. Madame Kismét inspected the work and seemed satisfied.

"Nice lacquerin'," she said, almost warmly. "I'm Madame Kismét."

"*Kiz-mā*? I thought it was *Kiz-met*," he said. "I read the sign."

"No," she insisted. "*Kiz- mā*," although she had never actually been to France. "It's *l'accent aigu. Aigu, aigu.*"

"G'bless ya," he said. "Johnson. Climax Johnson," he announced, like there was nothing unusual about his name.

She snorted in a backwards laugh like some people do and she was one of them.

"Thank you," she said to him. She waved her toes, allowing the cotton balls to drop.

"Yea, man, it's all cool." He stood up and she looked him up and down again.

"Tell you what…to thank you, y'understand…what would you rather do?" she asked, "have your fortune told…or hit this?" She opened her legs by flopping her knees apart and pointed to her crotch, which he could easily see. She didn't have to point.

"Can I get my fortune told and then see how that goes?"

"I knew you were going to say that," she told him.

"How did you know I was gonna say that?"

"Because I'm a psychic, that's how."

"Oh, yea. O.K. What do I do?"

She lifted herself up and stood, then walked over to a folding table disguised as something better because of its tablecloth. She sat down and opened her hands to him.

"Come here. Sit," she instructed. Climax walked over to her wobbly table and sat down on its other chair, a bit wobbly as well. She dealt out five cards, face down. She took his hands and placed them atop the cards spread out on the tabletop. She closed her eyes, although her eyelids fluttered a bit, which was her attempt to look entranced but came off as petite mal epilepsy. Climax reconsidered his choice.

"What? Do you see anything?" He lifted a hand to curl up one of the cards.

"Shh," she silenced him, and slapped his hand without even looking. and she continued to flutter for another moment. Then, "Ah, yes."

"Yes?"

"Yes. Definitely yes," she said.

"Yes, what?"

"I see you now."

"I'm right here, though.

"No, Mr. Johnson, I mean in my mind's eye."

"Call me Climax, please."

"No, Mr. Johnson. I'd rather not."

"O.K."

"And I see you wandering, searching…"

"For what? What am I searching for?"

"You are searching for relevance."

"They all gone. Haven't seen any of them since I was a l'il shitling."

"Not *relatives*," she corrected him, "relevance."

"What's that mean?"

"Shh."

"Damn, woman."

"You are searching, Mr. Johnson." She put her hands over her face and eyes.

"Yea, we both know that. And what?" She removed her hands and smiled, and when she opened her eyes, the irises were white — zombie movie white.

"Whoa!" he started. "You got them crazy sleepwalker eyes. How'd they get crazy like that?" He started to get up, but she grasped an arm and stopped him. She closed her eyes again.

"You will be in a horrifying accident soon, Mr. Johnson. You may even die."

"Didn't need that. Is it too late to change my mind? I think I want to hit that, instead," he said, pointing to her crotch.

"You are searching for the meaning of your life. Some reason for why you're important. And considering your immediate future, just in time."

"Yea, and hittin' that would be a good meaning for my life. And just in time, too," he said. "And keep them voodoo eyes closed."

"But you won't find that, I'm sorry to say."

"Let's just get back on that sofa. I'll find it."

"You won't find the meaning and importance of your life that you're searching for, I mean."

"Why? Why won't I find why I'm important?"

"Because you're not," she answered.

"Didn't need that, either."

She re-opened her eyes and after he flinched in anticipation of what he might see in them, he saw they were back to normal.

"That'll be twenty-five dollars," she said.

"I gave you three toes. bitch. Fuck you, Jack, I'm movin' on," he told her, got up out of the chair, walked out, and didn't look back.

"Don't you want to know why you're not important?" she called after him.

"No, ho," he answered back over his shoulder, "it's probably not important either. Bitch."

He climbed the stairs to the third floor, mumbling angrily the entire way. There it was, WEMD. "Country by day," the sign read, but didn't go on to say anything about the night.

Get a grip, ma man, Climax thought to himself. *Can't be goin' in here all jacked up. Chill. This is for a job. Fuck that bitch. Be nice. White man's world. Be professional.*

Park Bott was the Station Manager and Program Director. He was a loser with a job, which allowed him to outrank Climax in the world of losers. He was white, so Climax ran station managers through his blaxploitation barometer. There were no cross references.

Bott wore a pocket protector, but it held lollipops instead of pens. When offered, Climax shook his soft hand with a hesitant semi-firmness. He eyed the pocket protector and lollipops and all he could think was how he'd get the shit kicked out of him if had worn such a thing in the old neighborhood.

"Why do you want to work here at WEMD, Climax? By the way, do you mind if I call you Max?"

"You can call me anything you want if you hire me."

Mr. Bott smiled at him. He wore a dark blue tie and a dress shirt tucked into his black Sansabelt slacks. He had a little American flag tie tack. He had a baby-face and a sad attempt at a thin mustache.

"But why? Why here?" he asked. "What is it about this job that appeals to you?"

"Because, ma man, I'm looking for some meaning in my life," he answered, doling out the first thing that popped into his head. Madame Kismét's jibber-jabber was fresh in his mind. "I want to know I'm important in the world in some way. Ya follow what I'm sayin'?" Mr. Bott was shorter than Climax, so he tried to look him in the eye but only made it as high as his nose.

"Yes, Max, I do. Fulfillment, Max. I perfectly understand, and I applaud you for your uprightness."

"My what? I don't have any uprightness right now." Bott didn't understand Climax's misunderstanding, but depending on what Bott said next, Climax might walk right on out.

"Fulfillment, Max," Bott repeated. "That's sentiment enough to tell me all I need to know about you. I like you already. You have your priorities straight."

"My what?" Climax asked.

"Your priorities." Befuddled, Climax let it go.Perhaps priorities meant life's meaning and being important. Mr. Bott smiled at his nose and said, "You're hired, Max. I need a good man for the 42-for-you slot from 2 to 6. I have an instinct for good men. I don't think I even need to do a background check."

"No, ma man, I wouldn't think you needed to do that either." Climax looked at the clock on the wall. "You said 2 o'clock to 6? It's already 3."

"No, Max, 2 to 6—in the morning, after midnight."

"Say again?"

"Go catch a nap and be back here for 1:30 AM. I'll tell you what to do."

Climax left the third floor, engaging his tunnel vision as he passed Madame Kismét's establishment on the second.

"You owe me twenty-five bucks, asshole," she called out from behind her half open door.

"You have ugly feet and they smell bad," he called back to her.

He quickened his pace, but was stopped abruptly, bumping into a long-haired gaunt man on the first floor landing that opened into the foyer. The man had what seemed at least his own body weight's worth of metal sticking in and out of his face, nose, lips, eyebrows, ears, and forehead. When he and Climax bumped into each other, all the hardware clinked, even from places not visible.

"Hey, watch where you're goin, ma man," Climax said.

"Oh, sorry, man," the man said. "Hi. You were coming down from three. Are you the new disk jockey?"

"Yea, ma man, I be spinnin' from 2 to 6."

"Vlad," the man said.

"Johnson. Climax Johnson."

"Cool. And I thought I had a weird name."

"No, I like Vlad. It's sick."

"No, man, Climax is sick."

"They both be sick, ma man."

"Thanks, Climax," Vlad said, and he liked saying *Climax*. He reached up and cupped Climax's face in his hands.

"If there's one thing I can't stand, Climax, it's the unbroken continuity of someone's skin, glistening wantonly in its intactness, begging to be breached." Climax removed Vlad's hands.

"Not today," Vlad.

"No hole is too large or too small, Climax. I use beveled needles for your comfort and role-playing techniques for your mind."

"Not today, Vlad, I said."

"Do you have any fistulas I can use? There's a discount for those."

"Not to—"

"I've been sterilizing my equipment since 2002."

"Later, ma man." Climax turned and walked out of the main door.

"Later, Climax."

On his first night at WEMD, Climax learned what played at night after its "country by day." It was a strange music he couldn't understand—something called classic rock. It was stuff that had never played in the ghetto market, far removed from the hard wiring of whatever music appreciation had been instilled into his developing brain as a youth. Music, it seemed, was like language. If the engrams were not laid down at the beginning, a particular genre of music might as well be Chinese.

"Later, ma man."

"Later, Climax."

Climax had learned what WEMD played at night after its "country by day." It was a strange music he couldn't understand—something called classic rock. It was stuff that had never played in the ghetto market, far removed from the hard wiring of whatever music appreciation had been instilled into his developing brain as a youth. Music, it seemed, was like language. If the engrams were not laid down at the beginning, a particular genre of music might as well be Chinese.

The "42-for-you" survey was a list of 42 songs the Program Director felt were representative of what era or genre was important to feature that day. Actually, however, it was based on the fee-per-play royalties and the budget for the month.

The music appreciation engrams of Climax Johnson's brain, neuronal synapses of solid state forged in the ghetto furnaces of rap, hip hop, and urban R&B, began to erode and loosen a bit. His mind opened a crack.

That's when he heard it. The song that would make him love his work.

It was called *In-A-Gadda-Da-Vida* by a group called Iron Butterfly. In that *Louie Louie* manner, the title was a corruption of "in the garden of Eden," although he understood it perfectly via pidgin instinct.

Kingsmenesque linguistics aside, the real beauty of the song, to Climax, was that it was seventeen minutes long. The first half minute of it wasn't bad, he felt, even though he had no idea how the rest of it sounded, because the seventeen minutes gave him a chance to hit the stairwell for a smoke, visit the men's room for a smoke and other things, or even get laid, either in the men's room or in the stairwell. During the 2 AM to 6 AM slot, he could play it several times, for this time slot might as well have been in another dimension to the geriatric population that normally listened to this station by day. Country by day.

Climax went on several seventeen-minute breaks. No one noticed. The Program Director wasn't staying up to check on him, that was certain. All went well, as long as he was back in seventeen minutes.

One night it was a slow night at an ER in town. After the house favorite's signal had been crippled by FCC after-dark power mandates, the search for another station involved sweeping the dial on the old radio. The intern there happened to anchor into the signal of WEMD when he caught the iconic opening riff of *In-A-Gadda-Da-Vida* during his AM sweep. The song brought back nostalgic memories of pre-employment devil-may-care foolishness for the nurses and doctors there.

Before seventeen minutes had passed, things in the ER had picked up and never abated. No one had a chance to change the station by the time *In-A-Gadda-Da-Vida* came on for the fifth time. Even the patients complained.

"Please end that shit!" shouted a disheveled druggie in slot number eighteen.

A psychiatrist, consulted to see a woman with black toenails who claimed she saw stars in the sky that were sending her private messages of national importance, looked up the station's telephone number in an ancient telephone book with questionable stains. Climax had no phone in his broadcast room. All calls went straight to the Program Director.

As long as he was back in seventeen minutes.

On this particular night, he returned in nineteen, only to find the Program Director waiting for him.

"Climax?" the weasel most program directors were, fumed. In his peripheral vision he spotted an underage black girl spin around and escape back toward the stairwell.

"Yea, ma man?" he answered, buttoning up his trousers low under his hips.

Park Bott was befuddled, unable to choose which injudiciousness to address first. He watched the girl exit through the stairwell door and turned back around to Climax.

"You played *In-A-Gadda-Da-Vida* for seventeen minutes, and then it ended."

"They usually do end at the end, ma man."

"No, Max, it ended. It just ended. There was nothing. *In-A-Gadda-Da-Vida* for seventeen minutes, and then there was dead air for two. And I haven't even started to talk about how many times you played it. How many times, Max?"

Dead air, for those who have never worked radio before, is that mortal sin from which there is no recovery. It is the Shame of Marconi. Air's final electromagnetic entropy. The type of soundless sound that noise reduction headphones would turn into din. The Program Director raised his eyebrows, demanding an explanation.

"I said, how many times, Max?"

"Um, lemme see," Climax said, running his fingers through his hair. "At least once, maybe twice, I guess. Yea, twice. At least twice."

"The man on the phone told me five, Max. Five! And he was a doctor. Doctors don't lie, Max. Eighty-five minutes of Iron Butterfly, Max."

"That's better'n the other three hours of crap you make me play, ma man."

"Excuse me?"

"Hey, ma man, I'm talkin' Humphrey's Hermits, the Dave Clark—Five, is it? And what's that shit, the Moody Blue? Ya follow what I'm sayin'?"

"*Herman's* Hermits, Max. You were right about the five, but it's the Moody Bluezzzz. There's not just one Blue."

"O.K., so they're all moody. It's your station, ma man, so I'll play anything you want. But *In-A-Gadda-Da-Vida* was on the list, so I played it. Played the shit out of it."

"Again and again and again and again. Oh, and again." Bott said it as he emphatically slapped the fingers of his right hand into his left hand for each *again*.

"I getcha, ma man. I feel ya. O.K., I don't be playin' it more than a coupla times my shift from now on."

"You *don't* be playing it at all."

"You're taking it off the list?"

"Forget about In-A-Gadda-Da-Vida. Dead air, Max."

"Don't you think the audience needs a coupla minutes to recover after an oopus like that?"

"You mean *opus*, Max and no. Seventeen minutes of *In-A-Gadda-Da-Vida* and two of dead air. What is your explanation?"

"Chillin'. Seventeen to shuck and jive, two to chill. They're all just minutes. Seventeen of Iron Buddafly and two of dead air, ma man, I mean, what's the diff'rence?"

"Oh, I suppose…your employment."

"O.K., then, take it off the list. I don't have to play that."

"No, I'm taking *you* off the list."

"Say again? What list you talkin' about?"

And so it went. Climax had been fired for dead air. The Kardashians had made a career of it; even his man, Kanye, knew that. Climax was conflicted, but laughed himself out of his funk when he realized he was good at dead air. Really good.

Exceptional, in fact.

Now that he thought about it, he had been broadcasting dead air his whole life. His beginnings in this world had been dead air. His mother used to tell him that when he was born..."nothin'." He didn't cry, didn't move, just laid there, blue, so the doctor had to "beat it out of 'im." She said that the first thing she said to him in the delivery room when she finally heard him cry was, "I hear ya, ya li'l bastid." For Climax she had little prenatal care. She had chain-smoked the entire time until, at one of her rare prenatal visits, her obstetrician read her the riot act on smoking.

"What do you want? You want your baby to be stupid?" he asked in what he thought would be a sobering warning and call to action.

"That don't concern me none, 'cause he's gonna be stupid anyway." Her doctor had no answer for that. Dead air.

She dealt drugs in between her two tours as a POW herself in the War on Drugs and between each of her five — or was it six? — pregnancies. Then she never came back and that was on purpose, her whereabouts currently unknown. Climax couldn't even remember what she looked like. Dead air.

He didn't know his father except for his last name and what he had done. Two of his three brothers were dead, the other one just plain missing and that wasn't on purpose. His sister had married her pimp in a pregnancy love story that would have made a memorable dramedy.

His whole family before he had left home was dead air.

The only thing he was good for, he figured, was just seventeen minutes at a time. In fact, that's how long his job at the Dollar General had lasted. Al's Second Hand Tires even shorter. Burger King wouldn't even consider him because he was a filthy, dirty felon, the default party line on felons. But that wouldn't have lasted, anyway, because it takes over seventeen minutes to cook fries.

And so in the wee hours of the morning of his radio station shift cut short, before the sun rose, he walked toward the city bus stop and looked up into the sky, darkest before the dawn. Climax Johnson was an empty man with a missing vocation in a hollow society under a starless sky. As much an impact on the world as the stars before they had left.

Madame Kismét was right. He was not important at all. And she was right about another thing.

On the other hand, importance was everything that Keith Mills was about. This new character in Climax's story commuted either by limo, helicopter, or private jet. On the day that Climax Johnson crossed paths with him, each of them on opposite journeys through life, Mills was lounging unbuckled in the back of his limo with a Jack-and-Coke in hand. The limousine was moving at a considerable speed to catch a pre-dawn flight in Mills' private jet when an eco-friendly hybrid vehicle, weighed down considerably with a ballast of batteries, ran the red light and T-boned it slightly off-center. There were several spins of the limo, Keith Mills ricocheting inside like a pinball until he was flung through the separator window between the front seat and the rest of the limo and then out through the front windshield altogether, striking the driver on the way out who would have gone with him had he not been stopped by his seatbelt and an airbag. Meanwhile Climax Johnson, minding his own unimportance, was battered by the front hood on one of two-axle limo's triple Axels and then was impaled by a human projectile, the very important Keith Mills.

It was impossible to tell who had impaled whom.

"We're going to have to take them together," said the EMS respondent several minutes later. A crowd had gathered and was gawking. This was no ordinary gawk fodder. It was no ordinary traffic accident. Cars were stopped in four directions at the intersection. Even in this early hour additional ambulances had to sidewind their way through bike lanes, sidewalks, and stopped cars to reach Climax and Keith Mills.

"One guy's white and the other's black, and I still can't tell where one begins and the other ends," said the other EMS respondent, astonished.

"Guys?" asked a policeman. "You can tell they're guys?"

"Like I said, we're going to have to take them together. C'mon, let's get 'em in." After straight-boarding them securely, which took ingenious papooses in four different geometric planes, it took eight firemen to lift the entangled duo into the ambulance; two of them followed them in to secure them for the ride. One of them knocked on the glass to the driver.

"All secured. Let's move." The driver knocked back in acknowledgement and the ambulance began moving slowly through the cars and crowd, replete with warbling sirens, booming sound bursts of a lower register, and rapid chirps. Its lights tried to make sense of any type of rhythm, the reflections on the buildings providing an even more confusing visual backbeat.

"Wha- hoppen...?" Climax asked Mills, their faces only an inch from each other.

"Don- know...who are...y—?" Mills tried to reply, but then passed out.

The two firemen held on to them as best as they could for the intertwined mass of people they were. In and out Climax went, but Mills didn't regain consciousness the rest of the ride. On the way, an IV had been placed into each of them and they had been sedated.

Upon arrival to the ramp of the ER, a forewarned, forearmed group of doctors, nurses, and ancillary others met the ambulance with their IVs, catheters, syringes, and stethoscopes. They huddled at the back door. One of the two firemen inside opened it and as the door swung wide open, there was a collective gasp. One of the nurses vomited.

"We need two gurneys strapped together," hollered an intern. Shortly after, three nurses rolled the double gurney toward them, joined at their matching handrails with knotted rubber tourniquets.

"Oh, my God!" said someone.

"Holy shit," said another simultaneously.

"Mother of God," said yet another simultaneously, so it sounded like, "Holy shit of my Godmother."

"C'mon, on three," announced one of the firemen. "One...two...umph!" Up went Climax and Mills. Climax had just come to again and wailed out in pain. The same nurse who had vomited, having returned after regaining her composure, only vomited again. The double patient landed on the jerry-rigged double gurney. Climax wailed again and Mills was still unconscious.

Luckily it wasn't busy for the ER crew there that day, just like the night they had suffered through *In-A-Gadda-Da-Vida* five times.

An interesting collection of observations:

Madame Kismét had foretold that Climax would be in a horrible accident soon. In his brave foray against fate, Climax had played the aforementioned *In-A-Gadda-Da-Vida* five times — eighty-five minutes of Iron Butterfly, not counting the two minutes of dead air — initiating a series of events that would culminate in mayhem and calamity. The ER crew that was tuned in to WEMD heard the seventeen-minute opus repeatedly including the five insufferable guitar, organ and — especially drum — solos, until the psychiatrist, unknowingly involved in an astronomically unlikely coincidence consulting on the woman who had predicted it all, called the station to complain, which was the phone Park Bott had answered. This had provoked a philosophical dialogue about dead air that ended in Climax's termination an hour before his shift would normally end. Climax spent an exact number of minutes ruminating about his life of dead air. Had there been either fewer or more minutes in the reverie of his specious life pageantry or had there been an extra red light for the limo, or had the Prius not stopped at the Starbucks for a Café Latte Espresso, an entirely different drama would have ensued. Again, however, in persistent defiance of Madame Kismét's premonition, Climax began walking and at an intersection someone very important (his importance purposely vague in this narrative due to irrelevance) flew out of a limo that not only had struck Climax once, but had jettisoned this important man, Mills, into the very space occupied by Climax. This space was a tight fit and resulted in an ingenious fusion. Their combined medical triage took place at the hospital whose ER had originally called in the complaint about the excessive Iron Butterfly play, thereby setting into motion this entire mortality play. One could say it was Madame Kismét's fault or the fault of the Mills' limo driver or the fact that Mills had spurned his seat restraint; or Park Bott's impatience and zero tolerance for dead air or even the old green Prius that had run the red light and, still drivable, had fled, leaving a trail of battery hazmat.

But who could say for sure?

It used to be that one could say such things were written in the stars, but everyone had stopped saying such things. Besides, things written in the stars had to be rewritten every time a star fell out of the sky and self-immolated in a swansong through our atmosphere. For Climax Johnson there would be no such celestial script today, no *que sera* in the starlessness of this early morning's darkest hour before the dawn. This morning, everyone was on their own. The sky above offered only dead air.

Keith Mills regained consciousness just in time to hear the intern present him and Climax to the attending staff physician.

"Here we have these two gentlemen, a Mr. Keith Mills and an unknown black man who—"

"Johnson," Climax eked out.

"Excuse me?"

"Johnson...Climax Johnson," he said feebly.

"Mr. Ajax Johnson and Mr. Keith Mills." Climax let it go. Mr. Johnson was a pedestrian and Mr. Mills was in a limousine when a third car, in a Prius, so probably a Democrat—"

"No editorial comment, doctor," the attending reprimanded him.

"—when a third car became involved with both Mr. Mills' limo and the pedestrian Johnson."

"I see," the attending said, looking puzzled as he inspected them. "What the hell?"

"Well," explained the intern, "it seems that Mr. Johnson has suffered a compound fracture and that the better part of an entire femur has penetrated Mr. Mill's chest, just under his pericardium."

"So," the attending surmised, "into his descending aorta."

"It appears so, yes. As you might imagine, although this is probably just an orthopedic situation for Johnson, removing his femur from Mr. Mills would result in an instant exsanguination."

"Of Mills," the attending clarified.

"Yes."

"Oh, yes, I see." The attending's mind began to anticipate a dead end. Even if they were to get them into an OR—stocked, instruments opened and ready—there was no way they could prevent Mills' death upon removal of Johnson's leg from his chest. They would have to remove the leg, crack his chest, and then operate — carefully — all taking way too long. He'd be dead even before the heart-lung machine had been set up. The doctor looked for the rest of Johnson's leg — his tibia and fibula — and was unable to explain how they were actually behind Mills.

"What's that?" the attending asked, pointing to a round piece of glass sticking out of Mills' skull.

"I believe that's a piece of a cocktail glass."

"Ah." They both stood there silently, medically thinking medical thoughts that had never been thought before.

"Where should we go with this now?" the intern asked the attending.

"Room Seven," he answered. The intern sighed, prompting the attending to explain. "Even though Mr. Johnson's leg is tamponading Mr. Mills' aorta very nicely, the aorta's still leaking. Also, his spleen and liver are bleeding, too, and they will keep doing that, well, until. Has either of them been transfused?"

"No," answered the intern. "But they're both typed and matched. And if you don't mind me saying, sir, if we're going to Room Seven, it would seem to be a waste of good blood. But if you want to, they're both A-positive, even though we're still waiting to see if Mr. Johnson has sickle trait. In a way, Mr. Mills is being transfused, because Mr. Johnson's leg is bleeding into his aorta." He waited for some last heroic suggestion which didn't arrive. "So," he concluded with a single clap, "Room Seven?"

Room Seven, go to Heaven, was the saying. Room Seven was where a patient was parked until he died a death deemed inevitable. Gunshot-to-the-head victims, people who were drowned for over twenty minutes, human railroad roadkill who still had a pulse, and casualties who were still alive but were human Jenga games, like Mr. Mills, were extradited to Room Seven. The room was dark, quiet, and undisturbed, except for a stealthy medical assistant sneaking some vital signs from time to time, appraising the mortality countdown.

Climax opened his eyes. Mercifully, he had a considerable amount of morphine on board. He looked around. He had to strain to see past Mills, whose head was almost touching his. They were still conjoined on their double gurney.

Am I dead? he wondered. He looked at Mills, and wondered if he was taking one last ride with his fellow victim to the afterlife. Then he would pass out again.

He came to once when the aide was taking his blood pressure.

"Am I dead?" he asked her.

"No sir, you're not dead. But *that* guy," she pointed to Keith Mills, "is gonna be real soon. As soon as that happens, we're gonna pull you out of him and fix you up. You can thank your lucky stars."

Mills stirred. He opened his eyes. Climax's own eyes had adjusted to the dark, so he could see Mills very well. The man groaned.

"Hey, ma man," Climax greeted him with some effort.

"What—what's going on?" Mills asked. "What place is this? What happened? Am I dead?"

"No," Climax answered, "but they said you would be really soon."

"Well," Mills sighed, "at least I'm not dead yet." He splinted his body in pain. "At least I have time to make peace with God."

"Were you in a fight with him?"

"No, just an expression." He paused to groan again. "Hi, I'm Keith. I'd shake your hand, but I don't know where anything is."

"Johnson, Climax Johnson."

Climax could feel wet warmth surrounding the leg that had skewered Mr. Mills. No one had been able to even say which leg it was, but they knew it was his, because it was an African-American leg. They usually came in pairs, and there was another African-American one connected to Climax at some impossible angle.

"So, you believe in God?" Climax asked.

"Yes, I do."

"Oh."

"You don't?"

Climax paused to groan, himself. "Kinda, ma man," he answered. "Say, where's your family?"

"Where's yours?"

"I don't have any family."

"Oh, sorry…Climax, is it?" said Mills. Climax nodded, but then groaned. "I'm sure," Mills continued with some groans of his own, "mine have to move appointments, change plans, arrange for pet care, things like that to get down here to me. It would be nice to be able to tell my wife goodbye. I guess I don't have anyone, either."

"You got me, ma man," and Climax managed something close to a smile. "I'm staying with you to the end."

"Thanks, Climax."

"Ain't nothin'. Don't have much of a choice." He pointed down. Mills tried to look down at his chest, but stopped when he saw he had someone's leg coming out of it. "That's not supposed to be there, Keith, ma man."

"What's this in my head?" Mills asked, feeling the piece of glass with his fingers, cutting one of them. "Ow!" he said, and put the bleeding finger into his mouth.

"When it rains, it pours, ma man," Climax said.

"It's getting cold. Is it getting cold?" Mills asked. Then he laughed. "What a cliché."

"What's a cliché?" Climax asked.

"Like, oh, "death and taxes.' Guess I don't have to worry about that anymore."

"Which one?"

"Both of them," Mills laughed, which initiated a series of coughs that sprayed Climax's face with blood. "Sorry, Climax," he said.

"No worries, ma man." He looked at Mills' face. "You important? You a big shot?"

"Used to be," Mills answered. "Doesn't matter."

"Sure it does. You did stuff. Look at me. I ain't done shit with my life."

"Are you going to be dead, too, really soon like me? Did they say?"

"Nah. They said once you wrapped they was gonna yank me out of you and fix me up."

"I see. So I'm holding you up."

"No worries, ma man."

"Yes, I guess you could say I accomplished a lot of things in my life. Had a lot of things. Big house. Big cars. Money. Was very important," he said with an ironic smile. I think I can say I was fulfilled. Maybe even helped some people. But I guess I mainly helped myself, which is why I have to make my peace."

"Ma man! Compared to me, you —"

"Stop," Mills said. "Doesn't matter. Who's important or unimportant — doesn't matter."

"Why?"

"Because we all go out with a whimper. You later and me now, we all go out with a whimper." He clenched his jaw in pain, then relaxed again. "The stars, Climax. After they went away, I did a lot of thinking. Took some inventory. I don't know why, but I sensed my mortality. Like they were up in the sky holding my life together all tidy. Then when they went away, it was like it broke the seal. I became aware of being very vulnerable — guess that's where I became aware of my mortality. My wife and kids noticed and said I was overreacting, getting weird. Truth be told, Climax, I was just getting ready for today, it seems. Cramming for finals."

"Yea," said Climax, "I keep having a dream about taking finals, except in my dream I skipped all the classes and forgot to study."

"Oh, yes, I had that dream many times."

"Were you in your underwear walking to the test?"

"Y'know, Climax, the other day I asked my granddaughter if she knew who Bob Hope was. Muhammad Ali. Forget that!"

"Who's Bob Hope?"

"Doesn't matter who you are, who you were. We all go out with a whimper. Like we were never here."

"Like the stars," Climax said.

"Yes, like the stars," Mills agreed.

"Like dead air."

"Dead air? What's dead air?"

"The stuff that sounds good after classic rock."

"Oh, dead air—like on the radio. I see. Well, I suppose, yes," Mills said. "Going out in a whimper is like playing dead air. Here, anyway. But not where we're going, Climax."

"What's this we're?"

"Eventually, kind sir," Mills said.

"Where?"

"Actually, I can see it now."

"You can? See what?"

"Yes, and it's beautiful! And you know what?" he said, cries of pain becoming cries of joy, "everyone's important there. Everyone."

"Even people like me?"

"Especially people like you."

"You mean black people?"

"No, Climax, that's not what I meant. People...like *you*."

"Tell me what you see, please, I need to know."

"It is just lovely. Lots of light. Lots of beautiful flowers and waterfalls. And I see my mother, Climax. She's waiting for me. I'm not afraid."

"My momma," Climax blurted emotionally. "I would love to see my momma. I miss my momma. I know she misses me."

"And the women! What beautiful women!"

"Wait, momma. What about these women, Keith?"

"And my God," he added with a Bowmanesque flare, "it's filled with stars."

"Shit, ma man, forget the stars. Tell me about the women. I might be ready myself."

"You'll see, Climax. I'm there now. I'm in it."

"In what? In where? Are the women with you? I gotta know."

"Yes, Climax. Yes, yes."

"Where?"

"In the garden of Eden, Climax," Mills said, but he was drifting, so he slurred the words terribly. And then he closed his eyes for the last time.

The Savant

Jeremy Valentine, the adult son of the famous author, Thaddeus Valentine, had originally been a source of disappointment for his father at the age of two when his autism was first diagnosed. Like any parent who dreams of his child carrying on the family name and legacy, it was only a momentary disappointment, as fatherhood and love, the true results of reproduction, shoved the seductive if-onlies far away into the abyss, re-affirming for him what real life was all about.

Jeremy had a particular strain of the autism spectrum, one not well publicized, and thus Thaddeus began his obsession with autism and his written words about it that would win him his fourth National Magazine Award. Certainly not a scientist by any means, he nevertheless stunned the theater of neuroscience by describing a type of autism as extreme boredom due to sensuous impairment of time recognition, a temporal blindness. Some autistic children, he wrote, weren't out of their minds, but were just bored out of their minds.

His article, "Dyschronophasia," was first published in Discover Magazine, the only home he could find for it. This proved frustrating as the work had to be formulaically preened to the two thousand words allotted.

His son Jeremy was the only research he had done, and when other parents of autistic children discovered similarities in their own children, the Journal of Pediatric Neurology rewrote the Discovery Magazine piece, omissions replanted, as a prelude to the first official clinical study on the dystemporal syndrome, as it was labeled in the academic journals that followed. Studies into adolescence came next, followed by studies in adults and even those who had seemed to have "outgrown" their condition.

Cannabinoid receptors were initially prima facie receptors of interest, but it was soon evident that it was much more complex than this.

The good-time neurotransmitter, Dopamine, so important in both addiction and love, turned out to be just as crucial in the perception of time. Serotonin, GABA, norepinephrine, and another molecule from the spinal fluid, still named "Substance T," fit into the dystemporal scheme in some as-yet unidentified consortium.

The study of Jeremy, the son of the sentinel journalist on the subject, became the flagship investigation. His photophobia, though first to be a side effect of his medication, was soon identified to be only when in the presence of fluorescent lights. He began "speed listening" to music, claiming it was much more pleasant and he enjoyed melodies much more when music played at the equivalent of hundreds of RPMs. Yet playing a CD, with the sound bits flying at 44,100 per second, was noise, until he learned to listen to the melody from an analog recording of the original digital presentation, sped up manifold. Unable to dress himself completely, he nevertheless found a way to play a tape on fast speed into a recorder on slow, and then reverse them and repeat, until all that was left was gibberish. Anything slower he complained was too slow, besides being noisy.

And boring.

His dad found all of this puzzling and he began to put a lot of pieces together. There were certainly disorders of sight and hearing, blindness and deafness, respectively. There were those who could not smell or taste, anosmia and ageusia; diabetics with peripheral neuropathies often could not feel heat or cold or other touch sensations.

But the scientific world was strangely silent on the perception of the passage of time. If a fluorescent bulb blinking 120 times a second seemed to anyone with a time stretching syndrome to be a slow, relentless progression of sudden blinding flashes, it would be the optical version of a water torture. No wonder movies didn't catch Jeremy's interest, each frame, even at HD 72 frames a second—or even the digital equivalent of that—taking way too long to maintain interest. It was like being forced to page through someone else's vacation shots at one picture an hour.

Of course, conventional education meant nothing to autistic children like Jeremy. And not all autistic children displayed this savant tendency. But there were enough of them to create a division in taxonomy for the handicap, the new subcategory of dystemporal affect.

As the honorary father of dystemporal affect, Thaddeus Valentine was hard at work on the book proposal that would guarantee him a six-figure advance from any publisher. There would follow more scholarly books and even more famous authors visiting the subject. There would even be a fictional genre that would finally push vampires and magic into their well-deserved literary graves.

But Thaddeus was the original announcer of the condition to the world. Anyone who was fascinated enough to read books on the subject would certainly want to read his first.

It would of course be dedicated to Jeremy. It was to be an orderly chronicle of the discoveries made by Thaddeus regarding Jeremy, the orderly *chronicles* being an irony — a private joke Thaddeus was sure no one would get. It would be a tome of love to his son and to his wife who shared the journey. It would no doubt have a buying demographic that included anyone autism touched. With the rate of diagnosis increasing like it was, it would no doubt be a best seller. It would no doubt be seen on the shelves, in print, as well as be digitally available, by the following spring.

It would be delayed.

Somewhere between the outlines for Chapters Six and Seven is when the stars disappeared forever, and no one was quite the same after that. Not even Jeremy.

"My book," Jeremy said to his dad, "is it ready?" This is the way Jeremy referred to Thaddeus' book: *my* book. *Why not, indeed?* thought Thaddeus. It really was his book.

"No, Jeremy, it's going to take a little while longer." Jeremy sat at his tape machines, a stream of unintelligible RPMs playing in the background.

"Why, Dad?" he asked, while simultaneously switching tapes between the two machines he worked. Fingers that could not button his shirt deftly made the exchanges without difficulty.

"I really don't know. Remember last night?"

"I remember lots of things."

"Well, especially last night, when the stars went away. Remember that?"

"Yes, but I thought that was a long time ago."

"No, Jeremy, it was just last night." Thaddeus knew Jeremy, temporally blind, was incapable of nailing down any precise time points. "The publisher says that because everyone is kind of worried about the stars going away, it won't be business as usual for a little while."

"I love the stars," Jeremy said.

"I know, Jeremy."

It was true, he did love them. Thaddeus didn't know why, because he wasn't privy to what Jeremy saw in the world. Or above it. The stars had mesmerized Jeremy because they were as colorful and dazzling as any kaleidoscope. They were either red or blue, depending on whether they were moving away or toward him. But mostly red, since most of the universe tended to move away from most of the rest of the universe. For Jeremy, the cosmological constant had a color, and its color was red. The same neural aberrations that allowed him to swim very slowly in time also allowed him his Doppler vision.

"I saw them go away, Dad."

"Yes, Jeremy, a lot of people did. They were there and then they weren't. Just blinked away."

"No, Dad, they left."

"Where to?"

"Far away. Not here. And I saw them while they were leaving."

"How do you mean, Jeremy? They just left. It was very quick. Just gone."

"They were quick," Jeremy explained, "but not too quick for me." Jeremy turned the volume higher on the player.

"Could we turn that down, please?" Thaddeus asked. He was beginning to feel like he had a mosquito in his ear. "Thank you," he said when Jeremy complied. "Now, what exactly did you see?"

"They all turned red. Then they got smaller."

"Smaller? They were pretty small up there already."

"And pretty red."

"How so?"

"They were red. Most of them. Some were blue. The blue ones were coming and the red ones were leaving. But most of them were mostly red. And they turned redder. Even the blue ones turned red. And then they all made red lines and followed the red lines, and they went that way." Jeremy pointed up. "I keep looking for more blue ones, but I guess there won't be any more blue ones."

"Why not?"

"You're so silly, Dad."

Thaddeus Valentine was aware of the visual Doppler shift and the audio counterparts. What Jeremy was telling him implied that he saw the stars slowed down so much that he could actually perceive their redshift as they departed. In Thaddeus' research, Jeremy was able to count how many times a hummingbird's wings flapped in a two-second interval. Would it take much more to slo-mo actual photons?

Every night Jeremy would sit still at his bedroom window and dutifully observe, as if taking first watch for the world. He loved the Moon, but he really missed the stars.

A few weeks later, Thaddeus called for a person at the JPL named Dr. Michael Lewis, recommended by a journalistic friend, Martin Bragg. Thaddeus was told Dr. Lewis was no longer with the JPL. When he asked why, he was told Dr. Lewis took a leave of absence when the stars went away. It was a common occurrence in all professions, so when he asked when Dr. Lewis was returning, he was told simply that he wasn't.

"Ever?" Thaddeus asked.

"I'm sorry, Mr.Valentine, what exactly is this about?"

"I was told Dr. Lewis was my man."

"For what?"

"About the stars."

"You couldn't be more wrong, I'm afraid. Now, anyway. But tell me more. Maybe I can refer you to someone. But I have to tell you that any person here won't know any more than what you know already."

"About the redshift the stars left when they disappeared?"

"Excuse me?"

"There was a redshift. My son saw it. He can see really, really well."

"I've read your work, Mr. Valentine."

"Well, my son has autism."

"Whose doesn't?"

"Do you think all the autism is because of the stars?"

"Mr. Valentine, what's your point?"

"He experiences everything very slowly."

"So slow he can pick up redshift?" he asked. "That's what you're saying?" Thaddeus picked up on the cynicism.

"Among other things," he answered curtly. "If he can count hummingbird flaps, is it much of a stretch for him to see redshifts?"

"I would say, Mr. Valentine, that—yes—that would be quite a stretch indeed." He paused. "Still...interesting. It would have been nice to have had high speed film of the exact moment they disappeared to look for redshift. But, sorry to say, not only do we not have such a record, but there isn't even in existence a film speed high enough to show real-time Doppler shifts, irrespective of your son's—what should we call it?"

"Doppler vision."

"Quantum vision, Mr. Valentine."

"Never really thought to call it that."

"Yea, well, don't call it that, because he can't do that. He would have to see at quantum lengths." The man paused again, then, "Still, interesting," the man said again.

"And?"

"And...just interesting. Unfortunately, there isn't much we can do with that. There's a big difference between *interesting* and *interested*. You might want to contact the International Astronomical Union. They're the infidels who scratched Pluto off of the planets list, so let those maniacs deal with the rest of it. Thanks for sharing. Good day."

Thaddeus hung up the phone, stunned. A premier science entity — just not interested. He knew what his son saw. Jeremy had never been taught about Doppler phenomena, much less be able to understand it. Yet, how could he describe it perfectly like he did. It would make a nice follow-up for his next article, but it looked as if he would be relegated to Discovery Magazine again. Perhaps Scientific American?

Every night Jeremy would gaze out of his bedroom window, looking for the moon. The night after the JPL dismissal, Thaddeus walked upstairs and peeked into his room.

"How's the Moon looking tonight, Jeremy?" Jeremy turned from the window and smiled at his father.

"It's a little red right now, Dad."

Thaddeus entered and pulled up a chair to join his son at the window. One thing he knew: he would stay up with Jeremy all night tonight and night after night if he had to, so he might share the moment Jeremy would spot any blueshifts in the skies. Unless the Moon left first. Or until Jeremy became bored.

Whichever of these came first.

The Star Registry

Mr. Joseph R. Fritz, Trustee
In the United States Bankruptcy Court
For the Middle District of Florida, Tampa Division
Case # 065-090551,
4204 N. Nebraska Ave.
Tampa, FL 33603-4116

Re: Debtor, Star Conveyances and Registration International

"PERSONAL AND CONFIDENTIAL"

Mr. Fritz:

As one of Star Conveyances and Registration International's biggest customers, I would like to express how disappointed I was to hear that as a sole proprietorship it has filed for a Chapter 13 reorganization of its company. As you know from my previous fourteen letters, I have a lot invested in their services, notably in Ursa Minor, or the more pedestrian label, the Little Dipper, where I am just three stars short of owning the entire naked eye constellation, namely η *UMi* and Θ *UMi*, and of course Polaris, or α. I have to admit that I am relying on the Bayer System of star classification, but that agrees with the apparent magnitudes for the most part, which is what counts the most, in my humble opinion, when it comes to the affairs of the heart. I think I explained why I relied on the Bayer System in letter #6. The whole of Ursa Minor doesn't come cheap, as you well know. The stars already taken had to be bought from their current owners, but where money is no object, the stars can be had. I currently have offers in for the aforementioned η and Θ, and I expect their registrees to capitulate. As you know, the owner of Polaris has chosen to remain anonymous. I was relying on you to forward my message to him or her with my generous offer for it. Now I can't be certain of even that, and your total lack of response is beginning to concern me.

Let me explain yet again. The lovely exotic dancer, Ursula North, my "little dipper," my "little bear," is the unrequited object of my affections. I know she really cares for me by how nice she is when I go to watch her. I have been perplexed and chagrined, however, that she has been hesitant to engage with me in any outings, dates, meals, or even discrete meetings. To that end, I wanted to impress her in an "astronomically" big way, as it were. Imagine her intellectual surprise were I to present, instead of dollar bills or a purchase of another set of lap dances, an entire constellation deeded to her in your registry that will be copyrighted in a book placed in the United States Patent and Trademark Office! True, one might think it would be more impressive to present her with Ursa Major instead of Ursa Minor, but she is diminutive and might take offense at the implication. Besides, although I am a rich man, Ursa Major has just too many stars. Ursa Minor is no slouch, believe me, and any whole constellation would be impressive, especially one that spans 256 square degrees of sky! (Thank God I didn't fall in love with Andromeda, who usually takes the stage right after Ursula.)

Ursa Minor has the North Star, Polaris, for which I have been pining for a long time to buy, and it should be obvious that anyone with a surname, North, like Ursula North, should really have the North Star for their very own. Assuming I am successful in procuring it, I hope it is not lost on her that Polaris is a Cepheid Variable. It certainly is not lost on me that it is also called the Pole Star.

"How nice, how very nice," I imagine her saying to me outside of the dance club after she gets off work.

And now, just η and Θ short of my goal—and Polaris, of course—Star Conveyances and Registration International is no longer registering any stars. I don't know how much Ursula knows about stellar astronomy, but if she were to get her hands on a Bayer Classification catalogue, you could imagine my humiliation at falling three stars short in her eyes. Her starry eyes.

I know everyone says the stars are gone, but you and I know the truth, do we not? Where they are, I don't know, but I suspect you and the company you represent might. Along with the military, of course, and the people who killed Kennedy. After all, you're "in the business." As we all know, the stars all began at once in an explosion that set into motion machinations that would one day produce the loveliest heavenly body to ever rotate around a pole, my Ursula.

Sir, I implore you to help me complete my task, my constellational manifest destiny, when the company reorganizes, if not before. Please place me first on the buyers list when the conveyances resume. I must impress my Ursula. I must have my Ursula. I know there are other fish in the sea, as my mother told me while she was fixing my breakfast this morning, but there is only one Ursula North in the world and only one Ursa Minor in the sky. Please make them mine. Future generations, my own, depend on it. If the stars are in hiding, at least allow them this legacy. My legacy.

Yours truly,

Bubber Tant, Ursa Minor enthusiast

The Man in the Moon

After many years of a dark sky, as the first generation of starless children came of age, the world and the people who lived on Earth had come to terms with their special, solitary existence. The Moon, their only faithful companion in the heavens, continued to dance for the Sun, politely allowing the Earth's lead in each monthly sinusoidal ballet.

There were only three things in the universe: the Sun, the Earth, and the Moon. There were only three types of things in the universe: a star, a planet, and a moon. It was a time when everything about the universe could be known because all one had to know about the cosmos could be counted on one hand.

The quixotic storytellers will write that things became so bad, even the Moon couldn't bear it. One moment it was there like always, and another it was gone. It had joined the stars in abdicating a heritage shared with Man. This meant that Babel, the tragic tomb which was once the International Space Station—and now just as dead as the Moon before it—was the only sizeable thing left in space besides the Sun. And who knew how long the Sun would last?

It was originally predicted that the churches would fill after the stars went out; but they emptied. They fell into disrepair, and when the Moon disappeared, many risked the condemned structures to refill them once again. When it was obvious it, like the stars, would not return, the churches emptied a final time.

It had been fifteen years since the journalist Martin Bragg had asked his friend, Dr. Mike Lewis, what had happened to the stars. In a starless world, friendships that had lasted forever decayed, and theirs was no exception. After the Moon disappeared, Martin called his friend on the same mobile number for the first time since the time the stars went out.

"Why is it, Martin," Dr. Lewis asked, "that something has to disappear for you to call me?"

"I know it's been a long time. I should have called. You could have called, too, you know."

"True," Dr. Lewis agreed. "I'll save you a trip. I'm not even at JPL anymore, anyway. Martin, no one knows what happened to the Moon. Probably with the stars. But you know what? I really don't care. I haven't even thought about this stuff in over ten years. I'm a painter now. Not with an easel, mind you. I paint houses. No deep thinking necessary. And I'm happier for it, I'll tell you. So I guess you can just call me back when all the houses disappear."

"What about the Sun?" Martin asked.

"What about it?"

"Is it next?"

"If so, then it's a wrap, Martin. As it is, it'd have been better to never have had the Moon than to have had it and then lost it."

"How so?"

"Oh, you'll see," Dr. Lewis said, a hint of warning in his tone. "And for the record, my old friend, like the Moon, it's not better to have loved and lost than to have never loved at all. Love and the Moon, Martin." Neither man spoke for a long moment.

"How so, Mike?" Martin repeated. "Why would it have been better to have never had the Moon? I don't get it."

"Martin, get a nice job like mine. Less stress. Less worry. Instead of writing for the paper, get a paper route. Good for your coronary arteries. Now if you excuse me, I've got to finish painting this trim by tomorrow."

"Talk again some time, Mike?" Martin offered.

"Sure, Martin."

Before the Moon left, no one felt he could feel any more alone, but everyone found out that was incorrect. The starless children born into this icy solitude assumed loneliness to be the default sentiment of being, and the generation gap widened pathologically. The ones who remembered the stars suffered the most, however, and legislation followed a dark path into legalized suicide, involuntary euthanasia, and lackluster crime-fighting.

Before any of these things would matter, however, the masses of a mainly secular world now awaited the removal of the Sun and acted in their lives like it were imminent.

The way they behaved made anything left of civilization unimportant.

Lunacy: Fade to Black

"If the stars should appear one night in a thousand years, how would men believe and adore; and preserve for many generations the remembrance of the city of God which had been shown! But every night come out these envoys of beauty, and light the universe with their admonishing smile." Ralph Waldo Emerson, 1836.

Starlessness. *Moonlessness.* Whenever journalists typed the word "moonlessness," the spell-checker always changed it to "mindlessness."

It would become a world that would soon weather unstable seasons. Adjacent nations would gain coastal real estate from lower tides and the territorial wars that came with it. People on a moonless world would live in jet lag from the shortening days.

The nights went from dark to black.

Globally, the infertility rate would skyrocket due to worldwide menstrual dysrhythmia; it was only a matter of time before the population became unsustainable from generational attrition.

A whole new scientific discipline had arisen from the sudden disappearance of the heavens with the mission of finding out what had happened. It was a hybrid branch of science and the humanities that only the most brilliant and persevering could make their way through, for it required years of advanced education and expertise in astronomy, cosmology, mathematics, chemistry, physics, theology, sociology, and the behavioral sciences. It was a path paved in frustration, the path always ending in unprovable theory.

Ultimately, the conventional wisdom narrowed down to two possibilities:

Either, similar to what happened after the Big Bang, there was another episode of Cosmic Inflation, accelerated by vacuum energy, sending space-time and everything in it so many light-years away that even the relative distances between stars were a smidgen compared to the inflationary distance we had been pushed away from them. This would result in the stars suddenly absent, their light never reaching the Earth from such distances. For the camp who accepted this theory there was a race to derive the mathematics that accounted for the Sun still there for us and when it might be yanked away like everything else.

A new theory solved this in a way that also solved the Mercury and Venus enigma, explaining these two planets were on the opposite side of the Sun from the Earth. The theory stated that not all the planets needed to align on the opposite side, but just the two inner planets. If the new epoch of cosmic inflation began, instead of as a circle around Earth's orbit, as an ellipse whose one focal point was the Earth-Moon center of gravity and the other the Sun itself, everything else would go, along with Mercury and Venus.

Or, alternately, two branes crisscrossed, with our Earth and Moon in the crosshairs, such that we crossed over into another universe that was empty, our Sun cherry-picked along due to undulations of the branes themselves.

Of the two, the more romantic notion was the latter, but with a romantic corollary. Romantics became enamored with the Third Law of Sir Isaac Newton: a predominantly atheist world in another universe, completely alone, suddenly crossed over to a universe crowded with planets, countless stars, galaxies, and other astronomical bodies that used to be for us alone. *Our* planets, stars, and galaxies.

With or without its Moon, what a world of promise that would be!

Epilogue:
Newton Through the Looking Glass

It had always been starless here.

It was a beautiful, crisp night of uniform darkness that blanketed the shadowed half of this alien, atheist world, both chasing behind and receding away from the day, the metronome by which all life on this Earth bided time. The sky, cloudless and new-mooned, was pitch-black as every new moon evening had always been, a metaphor for the vague, unidentified loneliness of this world. Even when their moon waxed from new to full, it presented no more than a lukewarm spot in their sky, uninteresting and ridiculous — a fossil, only.

There was no such thing as Astronomy. There were no telescopes or astronomers. There were no astronauts; there had been at one time, but after the Moon program was over they all began selling real estate or cars, began sitting as vice-presidents of lending institutions, or became spokespersons endorsing corporate products and services. There was no money available for space-venturing once their Moon had been reached, which was the dead end of any space exploration. There was nothing beyond, nothing that required a science called Astronomy. There was no hope beyond the aspirations on terra firma.

Satellites were useful, but the space beyond them was not. There were no such things as Astrology, conjunctions, or celestial alignments. The sky really was the limit.

Life here was a hamster wheel unanchored to any cosmic perspective. Journalists covered the goings-on of people's lives and actions without connecting any dots. The President performed as his poorly-led country's chief executive. Philosophers were too self-referential, never venturing beyond solipsism. Seventh-graders moved onto eighth grade and sometimes they had to learn to deal with accidents and other bad things. Lovers made love, too soon instead of just in time; recklessly, instead of carefully; with the wrong people instead of the right ones. Balladeers sang empty songs that celebrated predictability in melody.

Stock brokers had no idea what was coming.

Terminal patients raised the threshold by which they judged their quality of life, accepting or declining heroic measures on a new rubric whose grading was curved downward. Zoologists were limited in species, since there was no guidance from above diversifying speciation. There were no seminarians, churches, religions, or evangelists. Schizophrenics saw no ghosts and savants saw no redshifts. There was no star registry, only the Moon crater registry, but all the craters were already taken; there had been no craters named after Jesuits, because there had been no St. Ignatius.

Their Man in the Moon looked down on those who navigate life via their plans. One never knows what is missed if it has never been, so the void beyond was seldom on the minds of the busy men and women there. There, it was better to have never loved at all.

Mostly, life went on in this atheist world, day after day, night after night, the void as much a part of their being as the air around them, and as much their companion as the love, hate, greed, benevolence, ruthlessness, and mercy that directed their motives and decisions. Always laughing at those who chose to look up, the universe was cold and uninviting.

It was a beautiful evening in this otherwise miserable, secular world. The sky, black like it always had been, sat empty except for this one lonely orb of life and its smaller sterile companion. A Sun shined for these two alone.

Branes collided.

When the sudden appearance of the stars, along with the planets and the trillion-trillion other things, effervesced into their night sky, it was the first throe of perspective for them.

Theology was soon to follow.

—SaBB—

Notes

Title
Starless and Bible Black was a line in a 1954 work by the Welsh poet, Dylan Thomas. From his "play for voices," *Under Milkwood:*

> *It is spring, moonless night in the small town, starless and bible-black, the cobblestreets silent and the hunched, courters'-and-rabbits' wood limping invisible down to the sloeblack, slow, black, crowblack, fishingboat-bobbing sea.*

The musical group, King Crimson, also used this for a title of one of their albums, issued in 1974. As a big fan of the group, I was glad to join them in highlighting this beautiful and powerful phrase.

Prologue
The geographical references, the city of Llareggub which sat under Milk Wood — that is, the town and the forested area above, respectively, are from the same Dylan Thomas work. (Llareggub is a reverse spelling of "buggerall.")

The Journalist
For those who demand a granular explanation of what is going on (or not, actually), this story gets that out of the way, but the ending of "The Journalist" establishes trouble ahead for those on a collision course with their own spirituality.

The President of the United States
The movie referenced is *Starman* (1984), directed by John Carpenter, starring Jeff Bridges and Karen Allen.

Starman:

> *"You are a strange species. Not like any other. And you'd be surprised how many there are. Intelligent but savage. Shall I tell you what I find beautiful about you? You are at your very best when things are worst."*

The quote from Laurie Anderson is from her 2010 album, *Homeland*, from the track, "Another Day in America."

The Philosopher
The movie referenced is the 1983 comedy, *Strange Brew*, with Second City TV characters Bob and Doug McKenzie (Rick Moranis and Dave Thomas, respectively).

Doug McKenzie: *"No point in steering now."*

The Malaise
For those who are non-Jehovah's Witnesses, the religious belief is that only 144,000 souls will be allowed in Heaven at Judgment Day. They are people described in Revelation 7:1-8 and 14:1-5: 12,000 from each of the 12 tribes of Israel, giving a total of 144,000.

Bourbon St., the Latin Quarter, Rembrandtplein, Kuta Beach, Rimini, the Skadarlija district, Taksim Square, and Puerto Banus: tourism party destinations in New Orleans, Paris, Amsterdam, Bali, Italy, Belgrade, Istanbul, and Spain, respectively.

The Astronomer and the Astrologer
Balthasar: one of the three Wise Men, along with Gaspar and Melchior. The Bible doesn't name them, but tradition has it these were the three.

Titus Flavius Josephus (37 AD – 100 AD): Romano-Jewish philosopher and historian contemporary with Christ.

Pythagoras of Samos (c.570-c.495 BC): *Musica universalis* (universal music, Music of the Spheres, or Harmony of the Spheres), refers to the movements of celestial bodies with proportions that correspond to musical measures. Pythagoras discovered the relationship between pitch of a note and the string length plucked to produce it. The orbital resonance of each heavenly body determines a relationship that produces a tenor of celestial sounds based on numerical ratios.

Harmony of the World (1806) from Ebenezer Sibly's Astrology, in A New and Complete Illustration of the Occult Sciences by Ebenezer Sibly: a heliocentric universe showing the planets' correct distances and the zodiacal signs with Aries beginning at the horizon and the other signs following in correct order. At the bottom are various references to biblical passages.

Zarathustra: *"Thus spake you,"* from the title of Richard Strauss' 1896 tone poem, *Thus Spake Zarathustra* (op. 30), based on a novel by Friedrich Nietzsche.

Tycho Brahe: Danish astronomer (1546-1601) who recorded his era's most accurate celestial observations. In 1566, he dueled with a fellow student over who was the better mathematician and lost enough of his nose that he used a metal prosthetic over it.

Copernicus: Nicolaus Copernicus (1473-1543): Renaissance mathematician and astronomer known for his heliocentric model of the solar system, igniting the Scientific Revolution.

Leonardo di ser Piero da Vinci (1452 –1519): Italian Renaissance artist, mathematician, and scientist.

A good book that tells the story of the pre-Renaissance fusion of science and art and their divergence is Jamie James' book, *The Music of the Spheres*.

The Seventh-Grader
The star referenced is the center star of Orion's belt, *Alnilam*.

The Lovers
The star, Polaris, is the tail end of Ursa Minor, also called the Little Dipper. Venus is both the Morning Star and the Evening Star, depending when and where it is seen.

The Balladeer
Prometheus was a Greek deity, meaning "foresight" (his brother, Epimetheus, means "hindsight"). Prometheus stole fire from Mt. Olympus and gave it to mankind, and the rest, as they say, is history. To punish Prometheus, Zeus chained him to a rock where an eagle pecked out his liver. Unfortunately, since Prometheus was immortal, his liver grew back every day for the eagle's daily visit.

Bile is a humor. The Greek physician Hippocrates (460–370 BC) theorized that human moods and emotions were caused by an imbalance in the four major "humors," or bodily fluids, i.e., yellow bile, black bile, blood, and phlegm. The yellow bile and black bile were responsible for aggression and anger, and depression, respectively.

The Patient
Mixed muellerian carcinosarcoma is a mixed gynecologic tumor that is both a cancer and a sarcoma. It has a low survival rate.

Stardust references the first stars of hydrogen converting to helium; then when hydrogen is depleted, helium undergoes fusion until all the helium is depleted; heavier elements are created and undergo fusion until iron. With core collapse and subsequent explosion, these heavier elements are cast out into the universe for reassembly into next generation stars and possibly complex molecules that, on Earth, became people.

The Life and Times of Climax Johnson
Bowmanesque flare is a nod to Arthur C. Clarke's sequel, *2010*, and the movie of the same name by Peter Hyams, a sequel to Stanley Kubrick's *2001: A Space Odyssey*. David Bowman's (Keir Dullea) description of the monolith in Jupiter space was, "My God, it's full of stars."

Fade to Black
The quote, *"If the stars should appear one night..."* is from Ralph Waldo Emerson's essay," (*Nature*, 1836), that is, you stop seeing things you have always seen.

The two theories for explaining the stars' disappearance are described. First, a cosmic inflation, similar to that within the first second of the universe, where the universe of space-time expanded in a trillionth of the first second after the big bang by a factor of 10^{26}. This mechanism, for purposes of STARLESS and Bible Black, means that an area of space beyond the moon underwent another cosmic inflation such that everything else is pushed so far away that light will take longer to reach back to the Earth than the expected life expectancy of the Sun. The stars are still out there, just "way out there" so far we'll never get a chance to see them. The Sun and the inferior planets, Mercury and Venus, flawed this possibility until it was theorized that the inflation began from an ellipse that excluded these two inferior planets.

The second phenomenon conjectured is that the membranes ("branes" in M-Theory) of two different universes made contact and mirror images of the Earth, Moon, and Sun were exchanged from each. This implies a parallel universe, one with just an identical Earth, Moon, and Sun, which would be an incredible coincidence in the scheme of creation, unless a quantum simultaneity of superposition were rolled into it — a cosmic Schrödinger's cat, until the branes crossed. The romance of the second explanation invokes Newton (For every action there is an opposite and equal reaction), building evidence for an exchange of our world for another.

Acknowledgements

I would like to thank my initial readers/proofreaders, Renee Niemann, Greg DiLeo, John DiLeo, II, Blaise DiLeo, and especially Phoebe DiLeo Maclachlan, for helping spot errors as well as make constructive criticisms. Thanks to Verónica Martínez for the cover design.

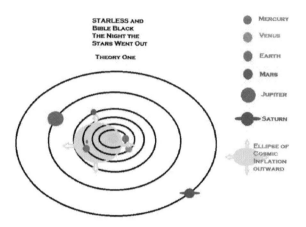

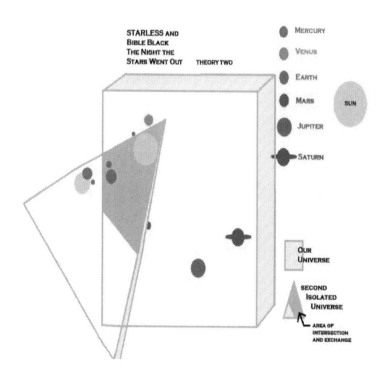

Made in the USA
Columbia, SC
23 March 2020